THE SPECTER

by

Jonas Saul

PUBLISHED BY:

Imagine Press Inc.
Ebook ISBN: 978-1-927404-61-4
Paperback ISBN: 978-1-998047-86-4
Hardcover ISBN: 978-1-998047-85-7

The Specter
Copyright © 2012 by Jonas Saul

The Decoy (Thirty-Three)
The Disappearance (Thirty-Four)
The Whole Truth (Thirty-Five)
Alex (Thirty-Six)
Parkman (Thirty-Seven)
Darwin (Thirty-Eight)
Aaron (Thirty-Nine)
Remains To Be Seen (Forty)

The Jake Wood Novels

The Immortal Gene (Book One)
The Immortal Target (Book Two)

Standalone Novels

'Til Death Do Us Part
The Drowning
The Woman in the Woods
The Threat
The Specter
The Mafia Trilogy
A Murder in Time
Frequency of the Dead

Co-Authored Novels

Collision Course (Written with Gary Ponzo)
There Will Be Blood (Written with Rania Stone)
The Soulless (Written with Rania Stone)

Short Story Collections

Twisted Fate (Tales of Horror)

The Specter

Twists of Fate (Tales of Hope)

Chapter 1

AARON STEVENS STARED AT the ferry and wondered how it was connected to his sister's disappearance.

She had been missing for two days, and the police had said there was nothing they could do. One cop even said she was probably still with one of her "customers." Comments like that have been commonplace since Joanne started dancing at the House of Lancaster strip club. Aaron detested what she did for a living, but she needed the money.

The ferry lit up, the lights on both levels turning on. A moment later, its engine came to life.

As the sun rose in the east, Aaron put on his sunglasses. He hated getting up this early, and today was worse than usual as he had pulled an all-nighter. He'd gone over the message from his sister in his head dozens of times.

Aaron, I'm in trouble ... after me ... ferry ... David Hornell ... vodka ... weeks ...

When Joanne left the message on his machine two days ago, the connection had been bad. She said she was in trouble. Someone was coming for her. The only other words he caught after that were *ferry, David Hornell, vodka,* and *weeks.*

At first, Aaron thought she was referring to some guy named David Hornell, who was gay and drank vodka for weeks, and now he was dangerous. But after using Google, he discovered that *David Hornell* was the name of the *ferry* that ushered people back and forth from the mainland to the Toronto Island Airport. After following up with the ferry and Toronto Island, it was only last night that he figured out *weeks* probably had nothing to do with seven days. He checked the little airport and discovered that Frank Weeks and his brother, Gary Weeks, worked there.

Vodka was the only word he still hadn't figured out.

As the airport employees entered the 5:15 a.m. ferry to the island, Aaron reasoned that he might never figure out the *vodka* connection. It could simply be the drink of choice on the night his sister called to ask for his help.

He checked his watch. The ferry would depart in two minutes.

As the airport workers boarded the ferry, he scanned their faces from the wall he leaned against twenty feet from the docks. At 5:30 a.m., another ferry would begin taking the regular passengers across every fifteen minutes until midnight, when the ferry service would retire for the day.

He recognized no one. Not a single individual looked at him either. Another nameless face in the big city of Toronto. Had anyone noticed him, they would probably assume he was homeless. He wore his white wife-beater top, a light, collared shirt unbuttoned over it, and loose shorts to combat the early summer heat.

The ropes were thrown off, and the ferry pulled away from the dock. The employees stood zombie-like in their early morning stupor, waiting to cross the short four-hundred-foot expanse of water.

Aaron pushed off the wall and stepped out into the light as the sun crested the edge of Lake Ontario. His polarized glasses reduced the water's glare.

He saw nothing suspicious. No one watched him. Although he had no idea what he was looking for, he had to be here. He had to do something. His sister was missing, and he would do whatever it took to get her back.

What happened to you, Joanne? Where are you?

It had been almost three months since they had talked. When he heard her message on his machine, the fear in her voice was unmistakable. Her pleading came through the static on the line. It drove a wedge in his heart that wouldn't come out until he found her alive.

The police had said they would look into it. They told him to let them do their job. They also said if she didn't return home soon, an officer would be in touch to get a statement from him.

The 5:30 a.m. ferry was pulling in to load passengers. He moved toward the access point on the dock and waited. As people gathered with small pieces of luggage, he took in the whole scene, just as his sensei had taught him years ago. Monitor everything around you, paying close attention to any possible threats.

His sister wouldn't have left a message like that on his phone and then disappeared without a word. Nothing was normal about anything that had happened in the last forty-eight hours. She hadn't answered her phone and hadn't returned to her apartment. The sister Aaron knew would never do that. That equated to Aaron assessing everything as a threat. He didn't know what the message meant, and he didn't know where the danger would come from, but he knew that he had to be on full alert.

Two deckhands tossed outlines, and another tied them to posts on the pier. The ferry docked and began letting passengers board. Aaron paid his fare, walked onto the ferry, and moved to a side railing where he could people-watch.

A young couple boarded with backpacks on, speaking to each other in French.

Must be on their way to Montreal, he thought, knowing that Air Canada and Porter Airlines both flew out of the airport.

The couple headed up the stairs to the observation decks.

A Coca-Cola truck and a white van with tinted windows moved forward to meet the ferry. Aaron wondered what the white van was delivering to the airport as it eased in behind the Coke truck.

After a few minutes of boarding, the ropes were pulled from the pier. Feeling no immediate threat, Aaron stared out at the water as the ferry got underway.

Is this what you did, Joanne? Is there something on the island that I'm supposed to discover? Did Frank or Gary Weeks do anything to you?

The crossing only took a few minutes, and the ferry slowed in preparation for docking at the island. Aaron moved along the railing toward the front, watching his back. He found it odd that he was following in his sister's footsteps, at least he hoped he was, and yet not a single cop had done the same as far as he knew. They had the recorded message. Today was the third day since anyone had seen Joanne, and they still hadn't even taken a formal statement from him.

When the boat bumped the dock hard, Aaron grabbed the railing. The two vehicles started their engines. The backpackers came down the steps while the rest of the early-morning passengers assembled to exit the ferry.

He stood in the shadow of the ferry's pilot house, watching everyone to see if anybody paid special attention to him.

No one did.

After the required wait, the ferry emptied, with Aaron walking off last. He followed the pack of people to the main building. The small airport was undergoing renovations. The temporary terminal building sat on the grass south of the runway. Aaron followed the group of people toward it. When he entered the terminal, a wave of cold air from the air conditioning blasted him.

He found an employee pushing an empty cart.

"Excuse me," Aaron said as he rushed over.

The man was just under six feet tall, but his slumped walk made him look shorter, his back rounded in fatigue. The man's name badge said Everton.

"Can you tell me whether Frank or Gary Weeks are working today?" Aaron asked.

The employee stopped and sized Aaron up, then met his eyes.

"Why you wanna talk to them?" Everton asked in a French accent.

"Old friends." *None of your fucking business.* "Either one

working today?"

Everton looked him up and down again, snorted in derision, and started away.

Aaron hustled up beside him. "Excuse me, why are you walking away?"

The man stopped again. "I gotta pull two doubles this week because of Frank not showing up for two days. Dat brother of his, Gary, he here, but he sure is lazy. Neither one of them needs a favor from me. You tell them when you find them that they owe me this time."

The man pushed away, yanking on the cart handle, and started off again.

Aaron kept up. "What do you mean, *find them*?"

Alarm bells rang in Aaron's mind.

Could Frank Weeks be missing, too? Is that why he hadn't shown up in two days? Was there a connection to Joanne?

"Frank hasn't shown up for work in two days," Everton said. "And he hasn't called in, eidder. Gary's been walking around like he's seen a ghost. He's trying to act normal, but I can tell the difference." The cart stopped, and Everton walked around to the front of it. "If you are their friend, why don't you know about Frank? Go find him and bring him here so I can go back to working my own shifts."

It was time to talk to Gary.

"Where can I find Gary? What department does he work in?"

"He's that guy that loads the luggage onto the planes. But you won't find him down there today."

Everton stared off at something over Aaron's shoulder. In defense, Aaron spun around, his hands clenching, always ready. No one was behind him, only a line of windows. Outside the windows, Aaron saw the white van from the ferry with tinted windows. Two men in dark suits and sunglasses escorted another man toward the van.

"Is that Gary Weeks?" he asked Everton.

Everton walked back to the cart's handle and sighed. "Why you asking me? I thought you was their friend? You don't know Gary by sight?" He started walking away. "I guess I'll have to cover more shifts this week. I know cops when I see them. Looks like Gary's in real trouble."

Aaron hit the doors and bolted outside, the morning sun feeling hotter after the cool comfort of conditioned air.

"Hey!" he shouted across the grass as he ran. "Excuse me!"

The trio reached the vehicle. One of the men opened the side sliding door and gestured for Gary to enter. Gary appeared to protest, then was shoved inside.

"Hey!" Aaron shouted again. *Something is wrong*, he thought. It didn't add up. It didn't look like two well-dressed police officers or detectives apprehending a suspect because the van wasn't a police issue. This was something else entirely.

After slamming the side door shut, each man moved to enter the van.

"Freeze!" Aaron yelled.

It was an old tactic his sensei had taught him years ago. "*Freeze*" always made people think it was the police.

It worked this time.

The man about to enter the van's passenger side turned and slowly removed his sunglasses. The pause was enough time for Aaron to reach him.

He panted, trying to catch his breath. "I need to know … where you're … taking Gary …"

The man placed his sunglasses back on and opened the van's door, ignoring Aaron.

Aaron reached out and stopped the door.

The man spun around to face Aaron.

"You can't be serious," he said, his voice dark like an unexplored basement. It sent shivers through Aaron.

"Who are you?" Aaron asked, knowing that if they were cops, they would have to identify themselves.

The driver had already gotten in and started the van.

"Let go of the door or lose the hand."

Aaron almost smiled. The last thing he needed was to be held on charges of assaulting a police officer. But he also understood the law better as he had recently been sitting for too many hours with his lawyer preparing his own defense on an attempted murder case. The cop, if that's what he was, had not identified himself, and he had just threatened Aaron with violence for simply touching the van's door.

Aaron held onto the door. "I don't take threats lightly."

As he spoke, the man turned to face Aaron fully.

Perfect, Aaron thought, *open yourself up to me and make your whole body a target. Your move, asshole.*

"Last chance," the man said. "Let go of the door and step away."

Aaron smiled as wide as he could, unmoved by the man's alpha male approach. He waited for the lunge, the grab, or the punch, but nothing came. He was prepared to block and attack, but instead, the man slowly moved his hand across his chest and pulled his jacket open a fraction to show him what was inside.

Aaron would've conceded defeat and walked away if it weren't for the fact that his sister was missing, and the only lead was Gary Weeks in the back of the van. Guns were something altogether more serious. The kind of serious that Aaron wasn't normally willing to tangle with.

But his sister *was* missing, Gary Weeks *was* in the back of the van, and Aaron didn't like being threatened.

Aaron's left hand shot out grabbed the man's right wrist —the one that would unholster the weapon—yanked it down, and twisted. At the same moment, his right hand released the van's door hit the pressure point at the base of the man's throat and applied the exact amount of force to cause prolonged choking but not enough pressure to collapse the trachea.

At times like this, he was glad he'd spent his entire youth working out, exercising, and doing his katas. Being a second-dan black belt in Shotokan karate and an instructor in his own dojo had been a lifelong dream. Having almost killed one of his students a month ago with his bare hands in a fit of rage had been bad for business. But it was times like this that his extreme skill wasn't tested; it was put to task.

The man slumped to the ground, clutching at his throat, gasping and choking, his face reddening.

The driver's side door slammed shut. Aaron spun and addressed the driver, who now stood beside the van's grill.

The driver had a cocked pistol in his hand.

"Step away, or I will shoot you in the iris of your left eye. You have one second."

The man's voice gave nothing away. He sounded colder than the air conditioning in the terminal. Like shooting someone in the face was as routine as eating ice cream on a hot day.

That voice persuaded Aaron to ease back, his hands raised chest high.

The driver helped his friend up into the passenger seat, keeping the gun trained on Aaron the whole time.

What the fuck is happening here? Aaron thought. *Who are these people?*

"Turn around and start walking," the driver ordered. "Do it now."

Aaron did, but not before scanning the terminal windows. At least a dozen people watched from the relative safety of the building. There is no way the guy would shoot an unarmed man in the back when his hands were raised. Not with that many witnesses.

The van door shut, and the wheels bit the grass as the vehicle raced away, headed for the ferry.

As they left, Aaron memorized every feature of the two suited men and the little he saw of Gary Weeks.

"Shit, now what?"

Chapter 2

AARON DIDN'T HAVE MUCH law enforcement experience until recently, but he could tell they weren't cops. They were something else entirely. Something dangerous.

He needed to find the detective in charge of his sister's disappearance and tell him what he just witnessed and how it was connected to Joanne and her cryptic message.

Once on the mainland, he jumped in his black Nissan Altima and drove along Lake Shore Boulevard toward Mississauga, where his sister lived in a high-rise building. The police station handling her missing persons case was the same one that booked him on the attempted murder charge months ago.

Now, on bail after his arraignment, he had certain terms to comply with. One of which was to stay out of trouble. Having a gun pointed at his face and smacking a guy around wasn't staying out of trouble.

He was also supposed to not use his hands. That was exactly what the judge had said, "Don't use your hands … they're lethal." After what happened to one of Aaron's students, he decided to sell the dojo to the Russians, who had been pressuring him to sell for over a year. Whatever form of martial arts they wanted to offer at the dojo was their business. Aaron knew he couldn't teach anymore after what happened. The money he got last week from the sale, which his lawyer had pushed through seriously fast, saying it would look good for him, was enough to allow him to stay unemployed for at least a year. After that, maybe he'd look into bouncing at a club, private security, or something along those lines.

He hit the Dixie Road access and started north, wondering what crackerjack cop would listen to Aaron's theories. He only hoped the cop would take him seriously because he was through doing it on his own. As much as he didn't want to admit it to himself, having a gun in his face really shook him up. He would prefer never to have that happen again.

Just south of Eglinton, he pulled into the Peel Regional, Twelfth Division office and parked in visitors. It was just after seven in the morning. He had no idea when detectives came on duty or if anyone would see him without an appointment, but he had to try or at least get the name of the officer handling his sister's case.

If the cops had already contacted me for a statement, I would have known who to see.

A pretty blond police officer in full uniform sat at the front desk, her hair done up in a bun. She looked all business.

"Excuse me," he said as he came closer.

She moved papers aside without looking at him. Then she picked up her coffee mug, took a sip, and set it back down before addressing him. She didn't say a word, only took in his tank top and open-collar shirt, no doubt assessing him as someone who broke the law. Who else would come in this early in the morning?

I guess you looking at me means I have the floor.

"My sister is missing. It was reported a couple of days ago. I have information for the detective handling the case."

"Name."

It didn't sound like a question.

"My name is Aaron Stevens."

She looked up at him. "No. The name of the missing person."

You could have said that, bitch.

"Joanne Stevens."

The officer lifted her coffee mug again and sipped louder this time, her right hand dancing on her keyboard.

"Detective Folley has the case."

"Could you let him know I'm here?" *Pulling a toenail off with pliers might be easier than getting you to help me out here, Cruella.*

"He's not seeing anyone at the moment."

"Just ring him up and tell him that Aaron Stevens, Joanne's brother, needs to talk to him. He hasn't even taken a formal statement from me yet."

The expression on her face made it clear she heard his exasperation.

"When I said that he's not seeing anyone at the moment, that's what I meant, as in he's free. No one else is in his office."

Egg and yoke on my face.

"Sorry, I thought you meant that he *wouldn't* see me," Aaron said, his soft explanation not removing the scowl from the cop's face.

She lifted a phone, dialed three numbers, and waited. Two uniformed officers exited a side door and walked out the front with Tim Horton's coffee cups in their hands. Numerous jokes about cops and donut shops raced through his mind. He stared at the woman behind the desk to take the smirk off his face.

She set the phone down.

"You don't have an appointment," she said. Then she grabbed a pen and paper and jotted down Folley's name and a number. "Call this number and book something with him for next week. He's pretty busy this week." She handed him the paper and lifted her coffee cup to her mouth.

"You've got to be joking?"

She stopped mid-sip. Only her eyes lifted to meet his.

"I mean, this is a joke?" He schooled himself to exercise caution, but school was out. "I've got information that might help in finding my sister. Why doesn't anybody want to hear what I have to say?"

"Sir, you're going to have to calm down." She stood up. "Call the number I gave you after you leave the building."

"What's your name and badge number? I know that's something, by law, that you have to surrender upon being asked. When this is all over, I will report it. I will tell them that I knew pertinent information about a missing person and that I just witnessed a kidnapping not thirty minutes ago, and you refused me. The guy had a gun and threatened to kill me. You told me to exit the building and book an *appointment.*"

He said the last bit in a snarl. He knew he shouldn't have, but he did.

Her face softened. After being arrested himself, held in jail overnight until the arraignment, standing before the judge, and being let out on bail, regular cops didn't intimidate him anymore. They were just doing their jobs, and he had nothing to worry about as long as he wasn't breaking the law.

A male voice behind him said, "Did you say you just witnessed another kidnapping?"

Aaron spun around and lowered into a half crouch. A moment before, no one had been there. Whenever someone crept up on him, his training took over. Years of training with a blindfold had fine-tuned his reflexes to lightning quick.

The man wore a plaid suit and an expression that went from morose to serious when Aaron spun toward him. His hand twitched toward his holster.

Aaron stood to his full height, resting his hands down to his side. "Yes, I did."

"You're going to need to calm down," the man said. "Can you do that?"

"Of course, I can do that."

"Why are you so on edge?" the man asked, setting his jacket right now that the tension had eased out of the air.

Aaron couldn't explain his training. It would take too long, and even then, not many people would understand. For years, he had sat in the center of a circle of martial artists, wearing a blindfold, waiting for his sensei to tap the shoulder of one of his sparring partners, who would then quietly step closer and grab an arm or wrestle a leg out from under him. Aaron would have to fend off the attacker by feeling, hearing, and fighting in the dark. His sensei had called it *alley training*. He always said he had to prepare his students for jumping in a dark alley with limited movement. Aaron remembered him shouting, "You have to learn to fight with your hands and feet, not your eyes."

"I'm on edge because I just had a gun pointed at me. The man said he would shoot me in the *iris* if I didn't move away from him and his partner."

The man leaned over to the cop behind the desk, who smiled crookedly.

"It's not a joke," Aaron said.

"Shoot you in the iris?" the man repeated.

"Who are you?" Aaron asked.

"I'm Detective Folley. I'm handling your sister's case and a few others."

"A few others?"

"It seems two other people went missing that same night. I'm checking to see if they're connected."

"What?" Aaron felt lightheaded. Had they made progress? How aggressive had they been? What's been discovered so far?

"Come with me. Let's talk in my office."

Detective Folley led the way down a corridor to the right and down another corridor. He opened a door with a plaque with Folley's name printed in gold.

Inside the office were a simple desk and two chairs facing it. Aaron was surprised to see a MacBook Pro on Folley's desk.

"Department funding must've gone up in recent years."

"Why do you say that?"

Aaron pointed at the Mac. "Those aren't cheap."

"That's mine. I don't use department computers. PCs break down too much. But you didn't come here to talk computers, did you? Tell me what happened."

Framed certificates and achievements hung on the wall behind his desk. A Rubik's Cube sat to the right of his large white desk calendar.

"You ever solve that?" Aaron asked.

"No, but I keep trying. I can get one color and sometimes two, but that's it."

Aaron picked the chair that kept him out of the morning sun's glare coming from the window. He crossed his legs, ankle to knee. He wanted this first meeting to be casual, even social, so he could get to know Folley, feel him out, and see how invested he was in his job.

"Start anytime you want," Folley said.

Aaron told him about the recording from his sister on his voicemail and how it led him to go to the island airport that morning. "I'm surprised this is the first you're hearing of it."

"Doing a little investigative work yourself, are you?" Folley asked, completely ignoring the comment about prior knowledge of the recording. "I have to caution you away from doing that."

Aaron nodded in an *I understand what you're saying* way and continued. He told him about seeing Gary Weeks being pushed into the white van and that as he got close, the two guys in suits pulled weapons and threatened him. He didn't mention taking one of the suits off his feet. If it came up later, he'd deal with it then.

Folley was jotting notes. After a moment, he leaned back in his chair and tapped the pen against his lips.

"Your sister has been missing three days as of today."

Aaron nodded and waited.

"I have to caution you again. It's important you listen."

Aaron nodded for him to go ahead.

"Vigilantism. Doing it on your own." Folley leaned forward in his chair and braced his forearms on the desk. "Do you know how stupid it was to address those men? You could've been shot. When I find your sister, what do I tell her then? Her renegade brother got shot searching for you?"

Aaron looked away. Anger served itself up, along with a twist of lemon-filled pain. The bitter kind.

"What's wrong?" Folley asked. "Why are you so pissed off?" When Aaron didn't answer immediately, he continued. "Talk to me."

"All right. I'll talk because it may help you understand how I feel and why I will do whatever I can to locate my sister." He uncrossed his legs and stood, pacing off the anger, willing his temper to cool. "My sister has been missing for three days. So far, no one has taken my statement or asked me any questions." He looked at Folley and raised a hand. "I know, I know, you get missing person cases all the time, and they turn out to be a weekend drunken binge or someone eloped. Well, that hasn't happened in Joanne's case. She called me. She was scared. No one was there for her, and now she's gone. I'm fucking concerned here."

"I know, and that's what we're here for."

"My other issue was her job."

"How so?" Folley asked.

Aaron faced him, his body a temple, rigid in the face of adversity, every muscle tensing. "I felt that since she was a dancer, a *stripper*," the word slipped off his tongue like one would spit a gob of saliva on the pavement, "her case wouldn't get the same attention that another one would."

"That may be perceived in the public, but that isn't how it is here. Our job is to protect human life," he tapped his desk with his pen, "as the highest priority, and that includes dancers, prostitutes, and ballerinas. You clear on that?"

Aaron nodded, walked over to the Rubik's Cube, and picked it up. "You mind?"

Folley shook his head, set his pen down, laced his hands behind his head, and leaned back.

Aaron worked the puzzle, using deft fingers to slide and twist quickly, honed by years of managing and manipulating every muscle and tendon in his body. He got his first Rubik's Cube in the second foster home he was shipped to and only lost it three years ago. It was the one item that allowed his mind a chance to settle when the world around him was chaos.

It took him just over a minute to solve the cube. He slammed it down harder than he meant to.

"If only life could be that easy," he whispered.

Folley said nothing, just stared.

"My parents took Joanne and me on a summer vacation when I was twelve and Joanne was ten." He angled the guest chair and slumped in it, defeated momentarily as memories assailed him. "We had it all planned. Northern Ontario, camping, fishing, lakes, sunshine, swimming, and ice cream. Joanne had even bought suntan lotion out of her allowance— I remember because of how proud she was of it." He paused to collect his emotions. He refused to weep in front of Detective Folley. "They stopped at the Petro-Canada on Highway 400, just north of Toronto, and we all went to the bathroom." Aaron glared at Folley. "Joanne and I never saw them again."

"What? What happened?"

"Don't know. We waited all day. We were young. We didn't think to check the car for over ten minutes, but it was already gone. I told Joanne that they probably went to gas up and that they'd be right back. They never showed."

"Did you ever find out what happened?"

Aaron shook his head in the negative. "A nice lady bought us an ice cream when she became concerned with Joanne's crying. I'll never forget her. She had long earrings and a wide smile. To this day, I can close my eyes and still see that kind woman's face."

Folley unlaced his hands and clasped them together on his lap.

"They separated Joanne and me. They said there just weren't enough people taking a brother and a sister. We tried to stay in touch, but they moved us so much that it became impossible. When I was sixteen, I ran away. I left the system and started searching for Joanne. It took over two years. By the time I found her, she'd gone through seven homes and been abused by at least three different men. She was a wreck."

Aaron clenched his fist and covered it with his other hand.

"I had been practicing martial arts for a few years by then and wanted to go and kill whoever had done that to her, but she said it was over. She begged me to do nothing about it. Do you get my point? Not only didn't the system help us when we needed it the most, but no one was ever accountable. I pulled her out and gave her a place to stay. By the time she got clean of drugs and alcohol, she started dancing in the clubs around Toronto. She's an adult, and I couldn't talk her out of it. But understand something about me. I searched for her all those years ago, and I found her on my terms. No one helped. In fact, I was pushed away by the system. Privacy and shit like that. Well, guess what? She's the only family I've got left, and I will search for her this time, too. Nothing and no one will stop me. I'm a private citizen. I pay my taxes and will come and go as I please. And if I find whoever has hurt my baby sister, they had better fucking pray you get there first."

He slammed his fist into the palm of his other hand to release the pent-up anger. He needed to be in his gym. He needed the bag to punch and kick for an hour. It was the only way to release the violence.

Folley nodded, concern in his eyes. "Your story isn't uncommon. I understand where you're coming from, and I don't want to belittle you or your passion when I say that you have to let professionals handle this. You have to try to step aside and let us walk in on men with guns. You do know where I'm going with this?"

Why did I tell him in the first place? I should've expected that response because no one really cares, do they?

Folley typed on his MacBook. His eyes widened, and he looked from Aaron and then back to the screen.

"I thought I recognized your name. I didn't connect it to your sister when I got the file, but your name was nagging at me. Then I thought I'd check our system to see if there was anything on your parents, and here's what I found."

Aaron leaned forward as Folley turned the laptop toward him. His mug shot from six weeks ago filled the screen.

"What's all this?" Folley asked. "Attempted murder?

And now you're in my office telling me about guys pointing guns at you. Is trouble just finding you, or are you searching for it?"

Aaron got up and headed for the door.

"Hold up," Folley said.

Aaron stopped without turning around. He waited.

"You want to tell me about this so we can be on an even keel, or do you want to walk away and make me think you're just a bad dude looking to even a score?"

Aaron leaned against the wall, facing Folley.

"A seventeen-year-old girl showed up at my dojo two months ago. She had been in the hospital for three days. Her face was bruised up badly, one eye swollen shut. Her right arm was broken in two spots, and four of her fingers had been split back and broken like pretzels. She limped into the dojo and asked if I was the owner of the gym. She told me that one of my students was her father, John Ashcroft and that her mother was still in the hospital. Apparently, he had started taking my classes two months before so he could learn new and exciting ways to beat his wife and daughter." Aaron paused to step away from the wall. "The system wasn't helping. No charges were laid. The mother refused. The daughter was too afraid. I did two things wrong when John Ashcroft showed up in his regular Wednesday night class. I made an example of him, and I went too far. I showed the rest of my students what breaking up the human body looks like and how easy it is to snap bones. When Ashcroft lay in a puddle of his own blood, I explained to the students that if any of them used this martial art for abuse, the same consequences would befall them. John Ashcroft is still in a coma, and if he dies, my charge goes up to first-degree murder. I don't know how my lawyer got me bail, but he did. My dojo went up for sale the next day, and it sold to a bunch of Russians recently."

"You're full of tales about the system not working in your favor. Well, maybe I can change that, but you'll have to do something for me."

Aaron opened the office door and said, "What's that?"

"Stay out of this, and let us do our job. You're too wound up. You're too close to this. Trust me that doesn't work. Give me your cell number. I will call you every day. I will keep you in the loop. The minute I know something, I will tell you. No stone unturned. Deal?"

Aaron nodded, knowing he could never agree to walk away, but at least it would calm Folley and let him focus on what he had to do. He recited his cell number and walked away.

"Stevens?"

Aaron stopped and stuck his head back in. "Yeah?"

"Sorry about your parents. They sound like shits. When I have some free time, I'll look into your case. It was only eleven years ago. Maybe I can find something out for you."

"I had a recording on my cell phone for two days from my missing sister. After a little research, I witnessed Gary Weeks being manhandled into a white van. Do you mean you'll *investigate* my parents like you're handling my sister's case? Sorry, I'm not trying to be rude, but you can't even solve that Rubik's Cube. Detective Folley, thanks, but no thanks. Don't need your help, and how do you even know *if* I want to find my parents?"

He shut the door hard and walked away. He knew that was uncalled for, but he was sick of the system, the promises, and the security it was supposed to represent.

He had other places to go and other people to see. Aaron would find his sister before the cops did, and Folley could eat shit.

It didn't hit him until he had already pulled out of the station that Folley hadn't taken his statement of what happened on the island airport that morning. Men had pointed guns at him, and the detective didn't file a report or send someone else to do it.

What the fuck are the cops doing anyway?

It was time to get serious. He had a court date coming up for attempted murder. Jail time was a probability. He had to find Joanne and help her out of whatever trouble she was in before he could think about his own future.

Without Joanne, his only surviving family member, he had no future.

Chapter 3

THE ANGER AT THE system's injustice brewed in Aaron like rancid milk, turning his stomach and making him physically sick. He had to do something about it. He had to find Joanne first and then talk her into leaving the strip club. Whatever was needed, he would do it.

After staying up all night to meet the ferry at the Toronto docks, Aaron left the police station and headed home to sleep. But sleep was elusive. He tossed and turned, his mind spinning possible scenarios, attempting to sew something together that made sense.

At just after four in the afternoon, he rose from bed, groggy and exhausted, did a fifteen-minute kata to loosen up his muscles and initiate better blood flow, and got dressed.

He grabbed his car keys and headed out. Ten minutes later, he was en route to the House of Lancaster. Someone must have seen something. He still had no idea how Frank or his brother Gary were involved with his sister. Now that he had seen Gary, maybe one of the girls at the club would recall him.

He pulled into a half-full parking lot.

Not too busy just before the dinner hour, eh?

A large bouncer stood by the back entrance. The House of Lancaster had a front door facing Bloor Street, but almost everyone used the more discreet back door by the parking lot.

Aaron walked through the back lounge area, which was always devoid of people but was filled with tables and chairs. He walked down a short hall, the kitchen's window on his left, the stage on his right. Ahead of him sat the cavernous seating area where men could drink and drool over the cavorting bodies of half-naked women or, in some cases, completely naked women.

The young girl on the stage couldn't have been more than eighteen, thin, undernourished, already wavering on her feet, no doubt due to alcohol, dancing to a Blind Melon song about no rain. She wore a thong and nothing on her breasts as she worked the pole. Five men sat in pervert's row, right up at the stage, two of them tapping the edge of the stage to the beat of the song.

He found an empty seat halfway to the back. Talking to the dancers about his sister would provide a modicum of privacy.

He didn't have to wait long. A tall black girl wearing a purple lace bra and panties approached him.

"Ya wanna dance, honey?" The dancers were on him before the waitress.

"No, a coffee would work, though."

"I'm not a fucking waitress," she mumbled and was off

to the next table.

Caffeine in his bloodstream was a requirement before he attempted to talk to anybody. He needed a clear mind, one not subdued by lack of sleep.

The only woman in the club who wasn't dressed like a dancer sat at the bar on his right. He waited until she turned his way and then signaled her with a wave. She got up and approached.

"What'll it be?" she asked.

"Coffee."

She walked away, her hips swaying as though hoping she was hot enough to elicit a tip.

It was a world Aaron couldn't get into, a world he didn't understand. Sure, he was male and all that goes with that, but random pussy was never his thing. He couldn't desire a girl just because she showed him her wares.

He rationalized that it was the same as meeting a girl in the library. What if she was sweet, kind, and had a great sense of humor? They decide to go for a coffee or even dinner, and then she drops her shirt and exposes her breasts, asking him if he still wants to go for dinner. It was degrading and unnecessary.

He had no illusion that the dancers were exposing themselves to acquire a date, but the analogy worked for him because that's how he felt about a woman's beauty. It was to be seen and treasured by the man who loved them, not to be shown off for a cheap thrill.

Men were visual. Aaron understood this. But a gorgeous calf muscle exposed from under a pretty dress or a hot smile mixed with long, flowing hair was what captured his attention. There was nothing remotely interesting to him about a room filled with women disrobing and offering lap dances for twenty bucks or whatever it cost.

The waitress set his coffee down and mumbled something. Blind Melon had ended, and the emaciated girl on stage cavorted naked to Def Leppard's "Love Bites." The volume was so loud he didn't hear the waitress.

He handed her a five-dollar bill. She took a moment to spill his change on the table.

He leaned up and spoke loudly. "Do you know Joanne Stevens, my sister?"

The waitress stopped fiddling with the coins on her tray and glanced at him. Something flickered across her eyes at that moment.

She knows something. She's seen something.

The waitress set the rest of his change on the table beside his coffee.

"Nice girl. But I haven't seen her in almost a week."

She made to walk away. Aaron grabbed her wrist to hold her a moment longer.

"I'm asking because I haven't seen her in almost four days. Were you working the last night she danced? Can you tell me anything about her?"

The woman stared at Aaron's hand until he released her. She met his eyes.

"Don't ever touch me again. The bouncers don't like that sort of thing." She collected herself, adjusted her shirt, and moved her tray—all gestures of nervousness. "Joanne never talked about a brother."

"We haven't spoken to one another since she started working here."

The waitress nodded and backed away. "Sorry, can't help

you."

She spun around and headed toward the bar.

Folley had said others had disappeared that day, too, but Aaron had forgotten to ask what he meant by that.

That'll teach you to stay up all night. You can't think straight.

A short woman in her thirties approached him, a fake smile creasing her lips. She sat in the chair opposite him and put her hand on his right leg.

Aaron jumped and moved his leg away.

"Sorry," she said and started to get up.

He put a hand on her forearm. "No, stay, it just surprised me. I don't get touched often."

She eased back into her chair, a weird expression on her face. Then he understood.

"What I mean is, I don't get touched *unexpectedly* that often. Usually, I'm more prepared. It just made me jump. It was nothing." He lifted his coffee to test it.

Not bad for a strip club.

She applied her fake smile again. "You wanna buy me a drink?"

"You wanna answer a couple of questions for me?"

Her face turned serious. "You a cop?"

He shook his head. "No."

"What kinda questions?"

"How about I buy you a drink, and you'll see. Only answer what you feel comfortable answering. Deal?"

She looked around the club. She probably examined her prospects and found only slim pickings as it was still before five in the afternoon. She nodded, her eyes showing the pain of years of abuse. His heart sank.

Joanne, this life is so not you.

"Gin and tonic."

She leaned back in her chair, crossed her legs, and set her purse on the table beside his coffee.

Aaron found the waitress two tables from the bar, talking to one of the bouncers. He waited until she looked his way to motion for her.

For a strip club that's only got maybe fifteen men in it, the waitress is lazy. She should work the tables, pass the drinks out, and raise the tips.

The bouncer and the waitress looked at Aaron simultaneously, the kind of look that told him he was the subject of their conversation. It wasn't just a coincidence. The waitress did an over-the-shoulder thing while the bouncer lifted his head.

Oh, no.

Hoping to diffuse whatever they were talking about, he waved with his hand, pointed at the dancer sitting with him, and used his other hand to pantomime drinking.

The waitress said something else to the bouncer and then started toward Aaron's table.

The thin girl on stage had finished her set. The DJ was announcing a girl heralding from Vancouver, here, live, for the next few days only.

System of a Down blasted out of the speakers about toxicity as the waitress approached his table. He had to shout it twice to be heard over the roar of Serj Tankian's vocals.

When he thought he had a break in the music, he turned to the dancer at his table. She fidgeted with the strap on her purse.

Maybe it's all related to the club? Maybe something

happened a few days ago, and everyone's living on the edge.

He looked for the bouncer but couldn't find him. Mentally chastising himself, he sipped half the coffee down. He needed to be better in tune with his surroundings. He needed to know where the bouncer was at all times now that he had their attention. His presence had been noted.

He leaned across the table and shouted, "Do you know a dancer named Joanne Stevens?"

The girl looked sideways at him and shook her head. "I don't know names. Only stage names."

"You gals never use your real names amongst each other?"

She shook her head.

Aaron found that hard to believe. She had to be lying. On stage, a long-legged, dark-haired woman did some kind of sexual gymnastics on the stage to the beat of Godsmack.

The rest of his coffee went down in one long gulp. He knew the caffeine rush would cause him to be super hyper. It affected him like a sugar rush. Drinks like Red Bull were off the charts for him. Only in extreme situations would he have an energy drink.

He needed to be more assertive as he didn't know how long he had left. Whatever the waitress told the bouncer about him could mean he would have an early exit.

"Tell me"—he leaned across the table—"what happened here three nights ago? I think it involves my sister, Joanne, and now she's missing."

The dancer leaned away from him. "You a cop?" she asked again.

"I already said I wasn't. We both know that if I were, I would have to identify myself."

"Well, I have no idea what you're referring to."

"Sure you do."

He waited. He wanted his confidence to rub in like a soft lotion. He wanted her to feel she knew *exactly* what he was talking about, and looking for answers was just as routine as dancing for another customer.

He could tell that she wanted to leave.

Then she did.

"Hey, where are you going? Your drink is coming."

"I have to dance soon. I'm up next."

"But what about your drink?"

"You have it," she said and stumbled away.

"Shit," Aaron mumbled under his breath. Nothing was going as planned. He could feel he wasn't wanted here. The waitress hadn't returned with the gin and tonic. As far as he could see in the gloom, she had vanished from the floor. He still couldn't see the bouncer.

His eyes followed the dancer who had sat with him for a moment until she reached a back door to the left of the stage, where she glanced back at him before disappearing.

Maybe he should leave and tell Folley what's happening at the House of Lancaster. Maybe a bevy of cops could come in and ask their questions.

Yeah, and maybe pigs could not only fly, but they could become ninjas and take out angry birds instead of the other way around.

A hand rested on his shoulder.

Aaron dropped off the chair by slipping his butt forward, his knees bent, until he was in a crouch in front of the chair. He stood to his full height and stared at the bouncer the waitress had talked to.

"You shouldn't touch me," Aaron yelled over the music.

"You threatening me?" The bouncer moved closer.

"No. Just stay out of my personal space. It's called respect."

"You gotta leave."

"Why?" Aaron asked, his shoulders raised, his hands extended in a questioning gesture.

"You're causing a disturbance."

"How so?"

"Asking questions about girls who aren't here. How do you think that makes the other girls feel? You some kinda creeper? A stalker?" He walked around the table to within a foot of Aaron. "We don't want creepers in here. You gotta go."

"Did you say you didn't want creepers in here?"

The bouncer nodded.

"Then why are you here? You're the one who snuck up on me and caressed my shoulder."

The bouncer was fast. He lashed out to grab Aaron's arm, where he would try to twist it up and manhandle Aaron out of the club.

But Aaron was faster.

He allowed his arm to be taken. As the bouncer twisted it around, Aaron spun with it, snapped his arm out, and gripped the bouncer's wrist in one movement. With the added torque of Aaron's body, the full twist effect spun the bouncer's arm like a windmill, pulling his upper body down with it. Using the bouncer's body weight against him, the force was enough to spin the shoulder completely in a circle, lifting him off the ground in a body flip. He landed on his back hard, Aaron still holding the man's wrist.

"I told you never to touch me. The simple act of touching someone against their will is against the law in this country. What I just did is called self-defense." Aaron released the bouncer's wrist. "Touch me again, and I will be forced to use 'as much force as is necessary' as written in the Canadian Criminal Code. Are we clear?"

The bouncer coughed a few times. He got to his knees and then pulled himself up, using a nearby table for support, collecting his breath. Aaron wondered why he had taken so long to collect himself. Could he really have hurt such a big man from a simple flip? Or was he waiting for backup?

The music stopped. On stage, the dancer looked bewildered. She used her arms to cover her exposed breasts and leaned against the pole.

To Aaron's right, two new bouncers moved in. In his mind, he had already worked it all out. The only problem was that with men this big and this ready to fight, he would have to hurt them, but he didn't want to. He didn't come here for that. Breaking bones and causing blood to hit the beat-down carpet under his shoes would be like a day in the office, but he couldn't do it. Too much attention. The police would come. Folley would hear about it. Maybe his bail would be revoked.

It was time to leave. Peacefully.

He raised his hands in supplication. "Okay, okay, I'll leave. But I'm warning you, don't touch me. The hand that touches me gets broken. I don't bluff."

He could feel the eyes of everybody in the strip club on him. He moved to the other side of the table to keep his distance from the bouncers and started for the door. He kept his eyes on them, hoping they wouldn't try something stupid.

Sure, they might regret it, but so would he.

A few steps from the backdoor exit, one of the bouncers shouted something. He turned back as they crowded him.

The man he had flipped shot his index finger in Aaron's face and said, "Don't come back here again. Got it?"

Aaron hated it when someone jabbed a fatty finger in his face. Bouncers always had that I'm big-and-tough attitude. *I can push people around just because I can.*

He knew he shouldn't, but it was just too tempting, and his nerves were shot.

Aaron gripped the protruded finger with his left hand and the offender's elbow with his right. In one second, he pulled the finger back, bending the elbow. The man gasped and dropped to his knees. Aaron secured the man's wrist, bent as far as it would go without breaking it, and nodded at the other two men.

It happened so fast that they were stunned into immobility. Then, both men stepped forward.

"Don't!" Aaron ordered.

The man on his knees below him shouted in pain as Aaron leaned into the wrist. Both bouncers faltered, wondering what the right move was.

"I told you not to touch me."

"I didn't, I didn't …"

"I was walking out on my own. Sticking your finger in my face is a form of assault. Being an asshole isn't your fault, though. For that, I will forgive you. Now, here's today's lesson, folks. Be careful who you *think* you can push around. You never know who'll be patronizing your little nudie bar."

Aaron eased off on the pressure. The bouncer on his knees breathed easier.

"I'm going through that door," Aaron said. "Nothing more needs to happen. But if I feel threatened by any of you, we will have to have a more serious conversation. Understood?"

The man on his knees nodded vigorously. The other two men didn't acknowledge him in any way.

Unfettered anger rose in Aaron. He had come here to see if he could find a friend of Joanne's, and all he got was kicked out and in a fight, putting him no further ahead. He wanted to smack the dumb looks off their faces.

Are you too stupid to see when you're beat?

Aaron jumped forward a foot in a sudden movement, and the other two men stepped back.

He released the man below him. It was over. Defused.

Aaron walked out into the late afternoon sun. When he got to his car, he stopped. Someone was crouched behind his trunk.

"Hey?" he shouted. "Get up."

The dancer who had ordered the gin and tonic looked at him but stayed behind his car.

"I can't be seen talking to you," she said. "Look the other way. Lean against your car. Do you have a cell phone?"

"Yeah."

"Grab it. Pretend like you're on the phone. Then you can talk to me."

The back door of the club opened. One of the bouncers watched him. Aaron reached into his pocket, grabbed his car keys, and opened his door. Leaving it open, he retrieved his cell phone from his pocket, mock-dialed a number, and held it to his ear.

"What's going on?" he asked after a moment.

"A very powerful man came to the club three nights ago."

"Who?" Aaron said into his phone. Then he held it away from his head and shouted at the bouncer, "I'm calling the cops."

The bouncer went back inside the club.

"I don't know who," the dancer said. "All I know is that he chose two girls. One was Joanne, and the other was Jan Elliot. No one has seen either girl since that night."

Joanne had probably called him from the bathroom of the club that night. The interference would have been a low signal from within the building, which added to the noise of the music.

"Can you tell me anything else?"

"All I know is that the man was British and had at least six bodyguards. He was very rich. I was having a smoke outside when they left in three cars."

"Was Joanne with them?"

He didn't hear her whispered response. Aaron leaned in closer. She nodded, her eyes rimmed in tears.

"She was my friend. She talked about getting out of this place. She wanted to get away and said she would take me with her. Joanne said she would help me put my life back together. And now she's gone, and those bastards got paid to forget that the British man was even here."

"Got paid? How much are we talking?"

"A hundred thousand dollars was left with the owner. Can you believe it? One-hundred grand. Just to keep his presence here anonymous. But I also think it was to buy Jan and Joanne because they never returned. The boss spread the money among the bouncers and a few dancers. I didn't get a cent. I'm fucking done with this place. It's been dead in here since. And who knows when the rich guy will return and I will disappear? No, not for me. Wake-up call, honey, a wake-up call."

"Are you saying my sister and Jan left with this British guy?"

"Yes, but I could tell they didn't want to."

The woman adjusted her legs in her crouched position.

"Is it safe for you to go back in there?"

"Doesn't matter. I'm done. I'm never going back in there. Not with how they treated you for simply asking questions about your sister." Her face darkened for a moment, her eyes wet and pleading. "You *are* her brother, aren't you?"

"Yes, I am. And I need to find this British guy. Is there anything else you can tell me? Did they have Ontario license plates on the cars? Diplomatic plates? Or were they rentals?"

"What's a diplomatic plate?"

The door opened to the back of the club. Four bouncers started across the parking lot toward him. They had weapons. Aaron saw brass knuckles in one hand and a hammer in another.

Shit's gonna get bad, fast.

"Get in my car. Now."

"What, I can't be seen with you …" she trailed off when she saw the bouncers.

"Go," Aaron ordered as he slipped behind the wheel. He turned the engine over and dropped the car in drive just as the dancer fell into the passenger seat beside him. The car's forward motion as he slammed the accelerator shut both car doors.

As he exited the parking lot, the bouncers were doing

their best to run after his vehicle.
   What the fuck is going on?

Chapter 4

"WHAT WAS ALL THAT back there?" Aaron asked.

"No idea," the woman said. She was still dressed in a body-hugging skimpy dress and heels. She looked over her shoulder out the back window. "Fucking hotheads."

The dancer rummaged through her tiny purse, pulled out a pack of cigarettes, and made to light one.

"Not in my car. No smoking."

Aaron hit the entrance ramp to the QEW, gunning the Nissan's engine to get to highway speed as fast as he could.

"I need a smoke," she said, the annoyance in her voice evident.

"No, you don't. Talk first. Then smoke."

"Talk?" She dropped the pack of cigarettes back into her purse.

The years of dancing and whatever else she had been doing to herself had been hard on her. Out of the darkness of the club, the sun showed her age. She had to be in her late thirties or early forties. Her skin had lost its youthful elasticity from years of nicotine abuse. The capillaries on her nose were already breaking from the benefits of too much alcohol.

"I need to know who this rich British guy is and why he would spend serious money to keep his presence in a strip club quiet. On the night he leaves the club, two girls leave with him and are never heard of again. Doesn't that sound fucking odd to you?" He snuck a glance at her.

"Of course. We're all scared he'll come back. No one knows anything. All we saw was him having a good time, tipping like crazy, and then he met with the owner and left with Jan and Joanne. That's all I saw ..." she trailed off as she stared out her window.

"Maybe he's a politician," Aaron offered.

"No. Too public. Other customers would have recognized him. I have a feeling this was just some rich dude. The kind that gets what they want."

Aaron dropped the visor to block the low sun. "Do you think the money he left behind was silence money for the two girls he took with him?" *My sister.* "Or maybe he simply has so much money that he *bought* them."

She didn't answer right away.

Aaron said, "And what was the big deal back in the parking lot? The bouncers usually just kick someone out and leave it at that. Why would they come out ready to rumble? Why would a professional bouncer in a reputable establishment bring the fight outside the club once everything had been defused? Something's wrong here."

A lot of things aren't adding up.

He applied his turn signal and changed lanes, moving into the express lanes to avoid the slower-moving collector lanes.

"Where are we going?" she asked.

"The police."

"Oh, no, we're not," she shrieked. "Let me out."

She tried the door, but Aaron flipped the child-lock button.

"What the hell are you doing?" he asked. "Calm down."

"We're not going to the police." She leaned into the passenger door, dropping down in the seat as if someone outside was trying to see her.

"Why not?"

"Because. I don't talk to the police. Ever."

"Today is a good day to start."

She lunged toward him and pounded on his shoulder with both fists, screaming, "Stop the fucking car. Stop the car! Stop the car!"

Aaron tried to fend her off while attempting to keep the car in its lane.

"Okay, okay," he shouted. He grabbed one of her wrists, tightened his grip, and twisted until she bent sideways and screamed in pain. "You gonna stop hitting me?"

"Yeah, yeah, let go."

He released her wrist. "Don't ever do that again," he shouted. "We could've been killed."

"Stop the car," she said, staring straight ahead.

"Tell me why you won't talk to the police?"

"Stop the car. Let me out."

They were coming close to the Dixie Road access. Once on Dixie heading north toward Twelve Division, they would encounter over a dozen traffic lights. She would be able to jump out at anyone.

"Just tell the cops what you told me," Aaron said. "Then I will drive you wherever you want to go. Come on, help me out. We're talking about my sister here. You said she was kind to you and wanted to help you. Help *her* now."

"If you don't stop the car, I'm going to show the cop my wrist and say you kidnapped me and that I'm being held against my will. That would be the truth. I want out, and you're not letting me go. This is called forcible confinement. I know some shit, and this is forcible. Stop the car. Let me out."

Aaron knew she had him. He couldn't walk into Folley's office with a half-dressed woman and try to explain this away. He knew enough about what happened at the strip club to tell Folley.

But one thing still bothered him.

"How did you know what car was mine? There were at least fifteen cars in the lot. Why were you hiding behind mine?"

He felt her eyes on him.

"I didn't *know*. Lucky guess."

"Bullshit."

He raced up the Dixie exit and turned north. The light ahead was red.

"Look," he tried one more time. "Joanne needs help. You know stuff. Tell me, were they drinking vodka? She said something to me about vodka. Is that connected in any way?" He slowed the car, exasperated. "Come with me to the investigating officer and tell him everything. Please."

The car stopped. The dancer manually flipped the lock

and popped the door open. She looked back at Aaron before getting out. "That wasn't part of my deal. No cops. I didn't sign on for that. Fuck you."

She jumped from the Nissan without another word.

"Hey," Aaron yelled, but she was already on the sidewalk.

A horn blared behind him. A row of cars lined up in his rearview mirror.

"Shit."

He hit the gas, the passenger door slamming shut for the second time by the car's forward motion.

He slapped the steering wheel.

"Where are you, Joanne? What's happening?"

He stopped at another red light, his mind racing to figure out what to do next. All he could think to do was talk to Folley and tell him what he had learned at the House of Lancaster.

He waited for the light to turn green. The red-light camera stood sentinel, ready to take pictures of any red-light runners.

A camera.

Could a camera in the House of Lancaster record people coming or going? Maybe Folley could get them to show him what happened that night. Or maybe it was all erased for a price?

It angered him that he felt so helpless. There was really nothing he could do. He held no official capacity like Folley and couldn't allow himself to get into trouble while out on bail.

Aaron realized that his hands were tied. He had to let the system find his sister in their sweet old time. Whenever they got around to it, he might get a call.

He clenched a fist. If they had found her body and someone could have stopped whatever was happening, had they worked a little harder, he didn't know what he would do. Having learned about Gary and Frank Weeks and talked to the stripper, he wondered how far ahead the cops were. What could they possibly be doing to solve this if he's out here getting closer by the minute?

That left one thing for him to do. Someone at the strip club knew something, and they were hiding it. Someone knew something, whether it was the dancers, bouncers, or the owner. He'd rather spend a year in jail and save Joanne than lose her.

He pulled out his cell phone and called Daniel, his assistant from the dojo. He needed more people on his side. He would warn Daniel of the risks and explain the downside. Then he would get him to call a few of the black belts from the gym and see who wanted to go to the strip club to get some answers.

It was time to start asking the questions the hard way.

Being a nice guy simply wasn't working.

Chapter 5

Nancy Demeers walked a block up Dixie until she saw a coffee shop. Dressed as she was in her blue hip-hugging dress, people would stare, but she didn't care. She had done what was asked of her. She would collect her money and leave Toronto. Maybe it was time to visit her sister in Halifax.

She pulled her cell phone out and called the number she was supposed to memorize.

It was answered on the third ring.

"Hello?" Nancy whispered into the phone.

"Speak."

The man's voice was deep, gravelly.

"I did it. I told the man what you told me to say. I made sure he thought his sister was taken out of the club. He knows exactly what you wanted him to know."

"Good."

"Can someone come with my money and pick me up?"

"Sure. Where?"

"I'm at Dixie Road and The Queensway in Etobicoke. I'll be in a coffee shop on the northwest corner."

"Ten minutes."

The man's voice gave nothing away. No emotion, no appreciation, nothing. It gave her chills, even though the summer sun beat down on her exposed back.

"You'll have my money?"

"Yes. We need his license plate number. Did you get that?"

"Of course." She recited it by heart. "There, you have everything you asked for. Did I do good?"

She wanted a pat on the back for a job well done. Some form of gratitude. But nothing was forthcoming.

"Ten minutes. Be ready."

"Oh, wait. There are two more things. He asked about the vodka."

"Vodka?"

"He wanted to take me to the police station to report what I know. I refused and made him pull over to let me out. I think he's on his way to the cops." She paused. "I just thought you should know."

"Okay."

The line went dead. Nancy dropped the phone back in her purse and crossed at the lights. She entered the coffee shop and saw all six customers' eyes on her.

Take it all in, bastards. You're the last batch of people who look at this body without buying me dinner first.

She was done. No more dancing, no more drugs, no more drinking. Most of all, no more hooking on the side to support her habit. She had enough money to settle down for a couple of years. She would rent a car and head to Halifax or maybe take the bus so she could read on the way. It had been so long since she'd read a good book.

In the car, she had been worried when Aaron had asked her how she knew his car. And he wanted to take her to the police station. She couldn't believe it. Her deal would have been off if she walked through the door to a police station. They had been explicit in their arrangement. No police. Only information. Talk to whoever comes around asking for Joanne. Make sure they're not cops. Find out why they're asking and who they are. The man with the money said he would decide how important the information was. Once she talked to anyone, there would be a large payout. Enough that she could retire is what the man had said.

She sat in a corner booth without ordering anything. The girl behind the counter kept staring at her, but she brushed her away, pointing at the other seat as if waiting for someone. Eventually, everyone in the coffee shop averted their eyes, trying to be polite.

She wanted a smoke, but everything in Toronto was smoke-free now. She could barely smoke in her own apartment. It was so strict.

Outside, the sun relentlessly beat down, heating the humid air into the mid-thirties. She thought about the heat that Aaron had brought down on himself by showing up at the strip club. She didn't care. She wouldn't. It wasn't her deal. It had nothing to do with her. All she had to do was tell him a story and then let her new employer know she did, along with the plate number. As far as she was concerned, her job was done, and she hadn't hurt anybody.

The man she met at the club three nights before sounded like he had a Russian accent. The man on the phone was curt and to the point, but she could hear his Russian accent, too.

So why did they want me to tell the brother that the guy at the club was British?

She had no idea what was going on, and she really didn't want to know. Before Joanne and Jan left work that night, they were all given a story if anyone came asking questions. She was told the next night that Joanne and Jan had quit and moved away after being paid off for their help. If her brother hadn't been close to her and didn't know where she'd moved, it had nothing to do with her.

A black Mercedes pulled into the parking lot. No one got out. She wondered if it was her ride.

The driver honked the horn.

Nancy got up and walked over to the car. The tinted window on the passenger side lowered an inch. She leaned down.

"Nancy?" the driver asked.

"Yeah."

"Get in. We have your money."

Nancy opened the door and slipped into the comfortable leather seat, the air conditioning hitting her like a fridge door.

"Very nice," she said.

The driver pulled out and got on Dixie, heading south toward the highway.

"Where to?" he asked.

"My place."

He looked at her and then looked back at the road.

"Oh, right, sorry. I live two blocks from the House of Lancaster. It's easier that way. No need for a car. I walk to work."

This little bit of information didn't seem to impress the driver. He sat rigid, watching the road, not open for conversation.

There was movement in the back seat. Nancy turned to see who was with them, but her vision went dark as something hit her in the face.

She slumped down and fell out of the seat, her butt hitting the floorboards as she screamed and flailed at her eyes. A fire of pain flared inside her head as her hands grabbed the object on her face. It felt like two knives were sticking out of her eye sockets.

Her mind raced, and her hand flailed as the pain rose higher to match her screaming. Convulsions hit her body, knocking her hands off the knife handles.

She curled up on the floorboards of the Mercedes, all ninety-five pounds of her, spilling blood and brain fluid onto the carpet, wondering what had happened.

Chapter 6

DANIEL WOULD CALL A few of the guys and meet Aaron at the strip club at nine in the evening. Their plan was simple. Aaron would ask to talk to the manager or the owner and make it known that if they were willing to tell them everything, Aaron would leave the police out of it. The boys would run interference if the bouncers tried to get tough again.

That left Aaron with three hours to kill, so he decided to visit his sister's apartment, hoping to learn something about her disappearance. Getting inside might be challenging, so he brought Smokehead Scotch, the superintendent's favorite whiskey.

Early summer flowers around the building's grounds provided a colorful invitation to the apartment complex. A green pickup truck sat off to the side with gardening tools in the rear. Four people in green shirts and shorts raked, weeded and cut the surrounding grass. At least Joanne had found a reputable building in Mississauga. It had twenty-four-hour security and was inhabited by professionals. Not bad for almost three thousand a month.

He parked in visitor parking, grabbed the Smokehead off the car seat, and walked up to the building's intercom. A little square digital window sat above a series of buttons. He located the superintendent's number and dialed it.

"Hello?" Dewanda's friendly voice answered. "Can I help you?"

"Hello, I'm looking to see if there are any apartments for rent."

"Hold on, please."

He waited, tapping his foot, looking over his shoulder at the grounds crew. When he turned to the front windows of the lobby, Dewanda walked by, keys in hand. She opened the inner door and motioned Aaron inside. As far as he could tell, she didn't recognize him yet. The last time he'd been to Joanne's apartment was early March, more than three months ago, but he hadn't seen Dewanda since Christmas time. He'd bought her a bottle of Smokehead then, too.

He stepped in beside her, and her eyes met his. A flicker of familiarity crossed her face, and she smiled wide, wrinkles forming across her aged temples.

"Aaron, you bad boy," she said, her smile moving to her eyes. "You tricked me."

Dewanda was in her seventies, weathered from too many years outside and losing her hair. She had never gotten a driver's license. Aaron had asked her last Christmas how that was possible these days. She explained that her husband had taken care of everything when they were married young. She had four kids, all grown up, and moved on. They had taken the superintendent job as a couple in their late forties when the building was built and never left. Her husband had died from a severe stroke a dozen years ago, but Dewanda still plugged on, taking care of the building as only she knew how.

She leaned in close. "What have you got there?" she whispered as if what he carried was to be discussed in hushed tones.

"Smokehead."

"Oh, really?" A conspiratorial smile creased her lips. "And what is that for? I didn't think you drank alcohol."

"It's for the sweetest superintendent in the building."

She played it up, always the character. Her head tilted back, both hands going to her chest. "Oh, my, you shouldn't have."

"I want to talk to you about my sister," Aaron said, his tone serious. He handed Dewanda the paper-bag-wrapped bottle of whiskey. "Do you remember the last time you saw her?"

Dewanda took the proffered bottle and motioned him to follow her. "Come to the office. We'll talk there."

Aaron followed her down the first-floor corridor and into the small office. He sat opposite her desk and waited for her to shut the door. She set the bottle on the floor behind the desk.

"Joanne has been a model tenant," she said. "We never get any complaints, and her rent is always on time. You two come from good stock."

Aaron nodded, a hurt feeling in his stomach. It was hard to hear someone else praise his parents, the same *stock* that walked away eleven years before, setting in motion years of pain for him and Joanne, more so for Joanne.

"But three nights ago, I received my first complaint about apartment 802."

Aaron leaned forward in his chair. "What kind of complaint?"

"Noise. But that's not all."

"What else?"

"The next day, water was seeping into apartment 702, directly below your sister's apartment. After repeated efforts to contact her, I had to gain access to her apartment."

"What did you find?"

"Someone had left the bathtub running on full. It was coming out so fast that it flowed over the top of the tub and soaked the whole apartment, eventually leaking through minor cracks in the walls and out onto her balcony, where it continued to the apartments below hers. The damage was minimal, but we haven't seen her since that night, so I still haven't told her that I entered her premises."

"Can you tell me anything else? What kind of noise were the complaints about? Anything specific?"

Dewanda shook her head. "No, just yelling, or more like screaming. It lasted five minutes and was so intense that a neighbor called me. Then it ended."

"What time did this happen?"

"Two in the morning."

That would have been after the strip club closed. So whoever the British guy was that she left the club with must have brought her to her apartment. Maybe she thought she could have a quick bath. They argued and then left without turning off the water. It was starting to sound like she wasn't kidnapped. If whoever she was with had brought her to her apartment, it would have been to collect her things or to stay the night.

"Wow, that's late," Aaron said. He was out of questions. There wasn't much else to ask. Maybe she left the message on his machine from her apartment. She sounded afraid. She could still be in trouble. Or she could be in Britain for all he knew, about to call him any day to say that she's traveling Europe for a while.

Dewanda frowned and fidgeted with her fingers.

"What is it?" Aaron asked. "Something bothering you?"

Dewanda nodded.

"Tell me."

She stared at him. In her eyes, he saw that she struggled with a decision.

"I'm not supposed to show you."

"Show me what?"

"Come with me."

Dewanda got up and left the room, Aaron on her heels. Down the hall at the end, a door marked *Maintenance Room* opened to the right. Dewanda entered it and then opened another door immediately to her left. The second door had no sign.

A man in a security uniform leaned back in a leather office chair. He nodded at Aaron. Aaron nodded back. He counted ten television screens in a row, all showing different parts of the building's grounds, inside and out.

"Wow, this is something."

"We keep it pretty private. We have security guards walking the premises night and day, but we always have someone down here monitoring the grounds." She motioned for the man to type something. "Bring up camera six from three nights ago."

The man in uniform typed on the keyboard. Camera six was clearly marked below its screen. Aaron's stomach turned at the thought of what he would see.

The camera blanked out momentarily and then back on, showing an image of the main lobby and the intercom system he had just used to call Dewanda.

"At 2:13 a.m., you will see your sister with two men. Watch closely."

Aaron leaned in. The camera counted down the five seconds to 2:13 a.m. Then Joanne entered the screen. On either side stood two men wearing expensive suits. She looked unhappy, her face a scowl, her hair unkempt.

The security man hit a button on the screen, pausing the image.

Everything to his core felt sick. He couldn't believe what he was seeing.

"Have you called the police?"

"No. Why would I? This only shows Joanne leaving with two men. There was a noise complaint from her apartment, but we don't report things like that. It could've been an argument with her boyfriend, and they left with her still upset."

"Have any police officers been by to talk to you or enter her apartment?"

They both shook their heads.

"I reported Joanne missing two days ago. She left a message on my cell phone. She sounded scared. She asked for my help, but the signal was weak. I couldn't make out much." He threw his hands up in exasperation. "As far as I can tell, the police have done nothing."

He headed for the door. He needed to tell Folley what was going on. Something had to be done. He also needed to meet Daniel and the boys at the strip club later because he had to talk with the dancer who helped him out earlier. She said Joanne left with the British guy, yet his sister is on camera leaving her apartment building after two in the morning.

"Aaron, wait," Dewanda said. "Do you think those men are bad men?"

Aaron paused at the door, and another thought hit him. "Please, can I ask you to make me a copy of that bit? I need to take it to the police."

Dewanda nodded to the security guard.

"It'll only take a minute," the guard said.

"What's going on?" she asked.

"That's what I'm trying to figure out." Aaron studied the two men on the screen.

The same two men grabbed Gary Weeks that morning at the Toronto Island Airport.

Chapter 7

CLIVE BARON LIGHTLY TAPPED the end of his cigar in the marble ashtray to save it for later. He still had over three hours before he landed in Moscow on his private 747. He listened to the engines as they thrust the craft through the night sky at 837 kilometers per hour, according to the TV screen that folded down from the ceiling in his private conference room.

Born in London, Clive had made his money in alcohol in his early twenties. His motto had been, *work hard to make your money, then get your money to work hard for you.* And work it did. In the eighties, he had invested in various dot com companies that shot up like a penny stock that struck gold. Later, he invested in various golds and metals while building his alcohol retail and distribution business, giving it a more international presence.

The first time he killed a man was in the mid-1980s. He

didn't have to kill the man. The guy had just pissed Clive off. And Clive had loved it. The power behind the ability to silence someone … forever. It held a certain lust that he hadn't been able to shake since.

Alfred Johnson, an American, had come to London to discuss import and export options. His ideas were too simple for Clive, almost elementary school simple. He told Alfred that he had wasted his time. The next day, Alfred returned with allegations of tax fraud against Clive. He claimed to have discovered that Clive was importing vodka illegally into Russia. Whether that was true or not, Clive couldn't have people running around sullying his reputation.

So he invited Alfred to a meeting that evening to go over re-opening their talks, which he thought was Alfred's play from the beginning. Alfred accepted. Clive calmly walked in the hotel's back door an hour before their meeting, climbed the stairs to Alfred's room on the eleventh floor, and picked the lock. He entered the room without being seen or making a noise.

Alfred was in the shower. Clive waited out of respect. He wore gloves and a hood to do his best to contain hair and other items that made a forensics team salivate. He reasoned that evidence of his presence would amount to nothing as he had joined Alfred in this very room two days previous to collect his jacket before they took a stroll along the walking streets of London.

Clive quietly opened the balcony door in preparation.

When Alfred stepped from the shower, Clive still waited. He needed Alfred dry for what he was about to do. Wet would only make him more slippery when he tried to manhandle him.

Alfred exited the bathroom, wrapped a towel around his waist, and shouted in surprise at seeing someone in his room.

Clive charged him. He did his best to minimize any bruising as he shoved and maneuvered Alfred up and over the balcony railing. Once Alfred was in free fall, screaming his way to the concrete one hundred feet below, Clive simply exited the hotel room, used the stairs to get to the main floor, walked the three blocks to his car, drove to their prearranged meeting spot, and waited for Alfred to show. His security men met him there and waited with him for over an hour. He called Alfred's cell phone numerous times, leaving long messages about how unprofessional he had been by standing him up, and then Clive drove home.

During the investigation, he was questioned briefly, but his story checked out, and Alfred Johnson's death was labeled an accident.

Clive never forgot how good it felt to not only kill a man but to get away with it. Times have changed since the eighties. Investigations have reached a new level. It's much harder to kill someone without leaving a trace. That's why mercenaries like Jackson and Hugh worked for him now. They're professionals unlike any others, ex-Mossad, responsible for infiltrations on Iranian soil.

"Come," Clive said at the knock on the door.

Jessica Nockler entered, her hand staying on the door knob. She nodded with her darkened eyes and pouting mouth. To look at her, you wouldn't know what she had been through, but Clive knew. He also knew how valuable she was.

"He's ready," she said. "The drug has taken the desired effect. He will be groggy for at least two or three hours. After that, he'll pass out."

"Carry on," he said and waved. He expected the phone on the conference room table to ring. Without Jackson or Hugh calling in a status report, he couldn't go in and begin to entertain Joey, his unwilling partner, during the flight to Moscow.

He knew they would call. They always did. Only when something had gone wrong, or they had to deviate from the plan, would they call in late. Which meant he couldn't miss the call.

Jackson and Hugh were the kind of men who didn't care for Mossad's current motto: Where there is no guidance, a nation falls, but in an abundance of counselors, *there is safety.* They stood by the original motto: *You can wage your war by wise guidance.* That's why they joined the Mossad— to wage war.

Rogue countries like Iran needed to be brought in line. Jackson and Hugh were involved in the bombing of the Iranian Revolutionary Guard's Imam Ali Military Base in October 2010. They lost a few good men in the ensuing explosion. The base was said to house long-range missiles, one of Iran's most secure facilities. It was the Mossad who discovered Iran's nuclear program before it officially became known.

The president of Iran, Ahmadinejad, was quoted as saying that Israel should "vanish from the pages of time," which translates to "wiped off the map." Jackson felt more should be done to deal with this clear and present danger, but there was too much red tape and insufficient action.

He gave up on the heart of Israel over a year ago and decided not to continue serving his country. Hugh followed him, and both joined forces as mercenaries for Clive, making four times the money they used to make and enjoying their jobs even more.

Recently, the Mossad director had gone to the US national security officials to hear them out on what the American reaction would be if Israel attacked Iran amidst American objections.

Just last month, Jackson had said to Clive, "Too little too late."

Clive agreed, but he also kept his true opinions to himself. He was happy Israel was slow to the trigger. If they hadn't been, he wouldn't have Jackson and Hugh.

The phone rang, slapping him out of his reverie.

He hit the speaker.

"This is an encrypted line. Speak freely."

"We have a new problem," Jackson said.

"Explain."

"We have encountered other people who are aggressively asking questions."

"What kind of questions?"

Jackson cleared his throat. "A brother of one of the strippers has been asking questions. Aaron Stevens."

"That's impossible," Clive said, trying to control his anger. They had been swift in their cleanup to control information. He had been there himself. How could anyone be missed? "What could he know? It happened too quickly. I'm not sure I understand the situation correctly."

"We don't know everything yet. He approached Hugh and me when we took Gary this morning. He touched Hugh and, within a second, had him on the grass, choking. I had to draw my weapon on him."

Clive stood from his chair. "What the *fuck* are you talking about? Did he drop Hugh? In public? Nobody drops Hugh. I've seen the kinds of things he can do. Explain to me what happened."

The door to the conference room opened.

"Everything okay?" Jessica asked.

He waved her away. The door eased shut.

"The brother has figured something out," Jackson said. "He was at the island airport this morning and tried to stop us from taking Gary. Then he showed up at the strip club and harassed a waitress and the bouncers."

"What do you mean, harassed the bouncers?" Clive paced back and forth behind the conference table.

"One of the bouncers approached him and asked him to leave. He flipped the 250-pound man onto his back. When he was leaving, he brought the same man to his knees in front of two other bouncers."

"And no one did anything?" Clive asked, his voice rising higher than he wanted. "Were the cops called?"

"No police."

"Good. Can you handle this? What do we know about this Aaron Stevens?"

"We had Nancy go with him. She gave us the plate number of his car."

"Where's Nancy now?" Clive asked as he stopped pacing.

"She's with the others in Casa Loma."

"Good. You've done well. This sounds like it can be contained. Can you get to the brother?"

"Yes ... but Nancy told us something quite disturbing," Jackson said.

Clive's hand tightened into a fist beside the ashtray that held his cigar. "What is it?"

"The brother, Aaron, asked about the vodka."

"What?" Clive couldn't believe what he was hearing. Impossible. How could it be? "Say that again. Repeat yourself."

"Aaron Stevens asked about the vodka."

"How. Could. He. Know?" Clive asked through clenched teeth.

"We have no idea."

"Then find him. Find out what and how he knows, and report back to me. I land in Moscow"—he looked at the clock on his desk—"in three hours. If you find out before then, call me at this number. Otherwise, call my home line."

"What about the strip club? People are wondering what's really going on now that Aaron showed up and demanded answers. They're scared. When Nancy's death goes live on the news tonight, the people at the club will run scared. They may talk."

Clive waited for a heartbeat and pondered his decision. Things were unfolding like a ball of yarn rolling down a hill. He had to contain this mess swiftly and completely.

"Clean it up. You are my clean-up crew, so clean it up."

"Are you saying what I think you're saying?"

"Yes, no survivors. I want absolutely zero trace leading me back to Frank, Gary, and the rest of them. That means the waitress, the bouncers, the dancers, everyone. Take them all out and burn the *fucking* strip club down. Do it tonight. Leave nothing. We can't have left a speck of dust behind. With the brother, find out what he knows and make him suffer, causing us further cleanup. Make him truly suffer."

"Understood. It'll happen tonight."

"Then get on a plane and meet me back in Moscow."

Clive ended the call. Jackson was a competent man, as was Hugh. He had hired Jackson to head his private army, and so far, he had surpassed all his expectations.

And no one will ever find out that it was all about vodka. It always was and always will be.

He walked away from the conference table as the 747 flew through mild turbulence. He opened the door to the adjoining bedroom and saw his prize.

Joey Riley.

He was lying in the bed on his stomach, ankles tied, legs splayed open.

"Hello?" Joey asked, his voice laden with the effect of the drugs.

Clive was instantly hard as he stared at the soft hair just starting to grow on the back of Joey's young legs and ass.

"Hello, Joey. How are you feeling?"

"Pretty good. A little lightheaded. Strange-like …"

"That's good, Joey," Clive said as he removed his shorts.

A moment later, he climbed into bed and did things that Joey would never remember because Joey wouldn't live through the night.

Chapter 8

HUGH STARED OUT THE windshield as Jackson got off the phone and hopped back in the van. Hugh hadn't talked much since the airport incident. Jackson was sure it wasn't because of any damage to his throat. The hit Hugh took damaged his ego, and now that they got the order to not only take Aaron Stevens out but they could torture him first, Hugh would be happy.

Jackson started the van and pulled away.

"We got the go-ahead."

Hugh grunted.

"The club is to be cleaned up … completely. We got the okay to locate the brother, learn what he knows, and clean him up, too."

"I clean the brother," Hugh said. "No one else."

Jackson entered the QEW en route to the strip club. "Understood. He's yours. But not before we find out what he knows."

Hugh smiled. "That'll be the fun part."

"We'll go to the club after dinner and clean it up around nine tonight. Then we'll go to the brother's home and ask him what we need to know. In the morning, our plane takes us to Moscow. Everything seems to be coming together after all."

Hugh didn't respond. He clenched his hands and stared out the passenger window.

"Don't worry. The brother will have his due."

"Don't mother me. I fucked up. It was unexpected. He got the jump. It won't happen again."

Jackson nodded at him.

"Fair enough. Just don't lose your cool and kill him too fast. We need to talk to him."

Hugh didn't respond. It was so infuriating to talk to Hugh when he got in one of his moods.

"You heard me?"

"Yeah," Hugh whispered.

Jackson drove toward the House of Lancaster. He considered how many people he would have to kill that night and then wondered what he would have for dinner first.

Chapter 9

Folley turned up the north end of Spadina Road and entered the parking area of Casa Loma, where half a dozen police cruisers blocked the public entrance. He showed his badge to a uniformed officer and was waved in. He parked his car near the front.

Casa Loma, in a unique spot, overlooks Toronto off Davenport Hill. It was built in a gothic revival style over three years in the early 1900s for the exorbitant cost, in those days, of more than three million dollars. It came complete with massive stables and a hunting lodge. At the time of its construction, with almost a hundred rooms, it was the largest residence in Canada.

Folley had toured Casa Loma with three different girlfriends over five years. He'd also investigated two cases of missing persons involving sightings at the castle.

In 1933, the City of Toronto seized the rundown,

unkempt Casa Loma for non-payment of back taxes. The city then called for its demolition, but that never happened. In 1937, the city leased it to the Kiwanis Club of Toronto, later known as the Kiwanis Club of Casa Loma, which opened it to the public as a tourist attraction. It was the first time the general public could walk its halls. Recently, Detective Folley heard the City of Toronto was to take over management from the Kiwanis Club.

Folley also knew that it had been used as film locations for *X-Men*, *Strange Brew*, and Jackie Chan's *The Tuxedo* over the years. It remains one of Toronto's most popular tourist attractions.

Not after tonight, Folley thought as he got out of his car. He closed the car door and breathed in the evening air, fearing what he would find inside the castle's walls.

He showed his badge again at the main door and walked past the uniform guarding the front entrance. He entered the main foyer and was pointed toward the staircase on his right by another uniformed Toronto police officer.

"The Scottish Tower, sir," the uniform said.

"I've been here before, but I don't know the rooms or the towers by name."

"Just follow the trail of uniforms," the cop said. "They'll direct you, sir."

Folley lifted his index finger in the air. "Got it." He started up the steps, marveling at their size. Each time he visited, he was always taken aback by the massive building, originally built to house one family.

"A different era, a different era," he mumbled. To live in something as big as Casa Loma today would require a huge income just for the taxes.

He climbed to the second floor and was directed down a hall to another set of stairs on his right. Areas were roped off, and uniforms guarded everything so a stray member of the public or an employee wouldn't enter the crime scene area.

He had gotten the call as he headed home for dinner. Dead bodies at Casa Loma. Come quick. Possible dead were his case files. As a professional courtesy, Angela Wheeler from homicide had called him. The same Angela was too independent for a man, too determined to succeed. The same Angela let men know in no uncertain terms that she was unavailable because work came first. The same Angela, who was the hottest homicide detective on this side of Nepal.

No one knew how the dead got up to the third floor when the castle was open to tourists. Folley knew there were secret passages throughout the building, with numerous ones leading to and from the master bedroom, so the murderers would have been able to handle the task, providing they had the blueprints. However, it happened. A massive investigation was about to occur, keeping Casa Loma shut down for a long time.

He reached the third floor and started around a corner to access the steep metal stairs to the Scottish Tower. With both hands on the thin metal railing, he negotiated the steps one at a time and lifted his head into the tower. It was filled with men in white coats and at least six other detectives milling around, talking, coffees in their hands.

For a second, he wondered if they were filming a scene for a reality cop show. Everyone dressed for the part.

The smell hit him. His stomach dropped. He caught a glimpse of the outside through one of the small windows. The Scottish Tower offered a panoramic view of Toronto. He approached a window for fresh air and saw the stone lion on the castle's peak lit up in the floodlights outside. Tiny dots of lights, Toronto at night, spread out toward Lake Ontario like a bed of glistening diamonds on black velvet.

Inside, the walls were disgusting, covered with graffiti by a youth with no sense of respect.

Any adult who can deface such a gorgeous building is actually a child.

Detective Angela Wheeler wore a long overcoat for the evening, her hair done and her makeup complete. Folley figured she had planned an evening out when she got the call. Or maybe she dressed up in heels to attend murder scenes. He just couldn't be sure.

She held out a small, uncapped bottle. "Here, take this."

"What is it?"

"Vick's Vapor Rub."

He jabbed his thumb and forefinger into the container and applied the jelly liberally to the base of his nostrils. The intense mint smell instantly replaced the heady, horrible stench of gaseous bodies. The tip of his nose numbed as memories of childhood sicknesses flooded back, his mother applying Vick's to his chest.

Angela sealed the jar. "Five bodies in total," she said, straight to business.

"Do you have IDs yet?"

"Yes …"

"On all of them? Already?"

"Yeah. Whoever did this wanted us to ID them right away."

"How?"

Angela gestured to the bodies lying in various spots on

the floor, all covered in blankets. "Each victim was killed in a slightly different fashion, except the Weeks brothers. Each vic had their driver's license stapled to their foreheads." Angela coughed into her hand and opened a notepad she'd been holding. "Follow me."

She leaned down at the closest body and lifted the edge of the blanket. "Jan Elliot, age twenty-eight. Appears to have been asphyxiated. Bruising around the neck indicates strangulation." She stopped and referred to her notes. "She worked as a stripper at the House of Lancaster. Hasn't been seen in three days."

Folley noticed how flat the blanket was over her chest.

"If she was a dancer," he pointed at her breasts, "I'm not trying to be a pig here, but …"

Angela nodded. "They were sliced off after she was killed."

Folley's face tightened. "*After* she was killed?"

"Yeah." Angela walked over to the next body and exposed the face. "Frank Weeks, age forty-five. Stabbed in the heart at least five times. Worked at the Toronto Island Airport."

Folley nodded. He was all too clear on Frank's place of employment. He suspected Gary would also be among the dead, too. Angela moved to the next body without pulling the blanket up. She pointed down as she read from her notes. "Gary Weeks, age forty-eight. Also stabbed in the heart. Worked with his brother at the airport."

Folley stepped back. His shoulder bumped into the brick wall of the tower. "Wow."

"You okay, Folley? You don't look good."

"It's … this case just got a lot bigger."

"How so?"

"I talked to a guy this morning that saw Gary get grabbed by two guys in a white van. He approached them, tried to stop it, and reportedly got a gun shoved in his face for his trouble."

"We're going to need to talk to this guy. What's his name?"

She poised a pen over her notebook. Folley knew the case just slipped through his fingers. No one challenged Angela. She made steel appear weak. But she did say, *We're going to need to talk to this guy.*

"Aaron Stevens."

She stopped writing and looked at him, one eyebrow cocked high on her forehead.

"Stevens?" she asked.

Folley nodded. Then he connected it. "Don't tell me Joanne is here."

By the expression on Angela's face, he knew that under one of the remaining two blankets lay Joanne Stevens, sister to Aaron Stevens. He wondered how Aaron would take the news. He remembered their conversation in his office that morning about how the system hadn't worked for his family. Nobody ever stepped up to the plate for the Stevens family, and now Joanne had been murdered. He didn't want to be the one who told Aaron but knew he would have no choice. It was his case. They would need a positive ID on the body from a family member.

Or maybe homicide will take it from me.

"You were working on the Stevens case."

It wasn't a question. She knew. That's why she called Folley in.

"Yes. Aaron Stevens reported his sister missing a few days ago. He claimed to have seen Gary abducted at gunpoint this morning. He could even ID the perps. He said it was all connected. I guess he had no idea just how connected."

"I want to talk to Aaron ASAP. Can you call him? Get him to meet us at the station?"

"I'll call him, but be prepared; he's pretty fired up about finding his sister. Alive."

Angela nodded in understanding. "We've dealt with his kind before. But I want to know what made him feel it's all connected. Why was he at the airport this morning?" She stopped and stared at Folley. "How well do you know Aaron? Is there any chance he's involved in any way, and when he talked to you this morning, was it a cry for help? Maybe he's in over his head?"

Folley thought about it for a second and then shook his head. "No way. He came into the police station this morning because he was angry more wasn't being done to find his sister. I don't envy the person who has to tell him. How did she die? Any idea?"

Angela studied her notes. "Joanne Stevens, age twenty-two, was beaten with something bigger than a fist, more like a baseball bat. Then she was stabbed in the mouth, the blade coming out the back of her neck. It was a thick blade, slicing into her spine from the front." Angela said this without emotion as if reading baseball scores from the daily sports section. She pointed to the fifth blanket. "Nancy Demeers, age thirty-five, stabbed in each eye and then, after she was already dead, knifed in her vagina."

"Her vagina?" Folley asked, aghast. "What the *fuck*?"

"She still has the knife inside her. Joanne is missing both

breasts, too. They were sliced off after she died, and Jan Elliot is missing all her fingers and toes. Whoever did this hates women because the Weeks brothers were just stabbed in the heart and left alone after they died." She paused. "But there's something else that's strange."

Folley's empty stomach turned, the crazy feeling of the Vicks dangling from his nose making him think he looked like a warped clown. At least all the bodies were wrapped in blankets. Otherwise, he might have vomited if he'd seen what Angela had just described. Maybe that was why *she* handled homicides, and *he* didn't. It all came down to the stomach and how much it could handle.

"What's stranger than what you just described?" Folley asked.

She slipped her notepad back inside her overcoat's side pocket. "Each body had a crucifix placed on their chest, directly over the victim's heart. It came across to me like it was a religious killing. But then we've got the anger toward women angle." She rolled her eyes and shook her head. "Stranger than fiction."

Folley wondered how Angela Wheeler kept it together to do her job night and day.

"Hey, Folley," she called after him as he headed for the stairs.

"Yeah?"

"You gonna talk to the Stevens guy?"

"Yes."

"We'll need him for a positive ID. How many of these people were your cases?"

"Joanne and Jan. They both worked at the House of Lancaster. I have a feeling Nancy did, too. Also, the Weeks brothers' cases just hit my desk. I had plans to take Aaron's statement tomorrow regarding Gary's abduction this morning at the airport. So, I guess, all of them."

Angela coughed into her elbow. "We could use you on this."

"How? I'm not homicide."

"I know. But all these cases are—sorry, *were*—yours. You've met Aaron. You were going to call him about Gary. You're pretty tight with this. So, what do you say? Help me out here. Get Aaron's statement. Get him to do the positive ID on Joanne and then sweat him a little. Find out what made him go to the airport this morning. Report to me directly. I'll file the request to transfer you for this case. Don't worry, I'll get the okay. You in?"

Folley knew Aaron. He had seen his passion, felt his anger. Maybe he could insulate the tough homicide detectives from Aaron and vice versa.

"Do it," he said. "File the transfer. *I'm yours*, as Jason Mraz says."

"Jason who?"

He was drawn to Angela's gorgeous blue eyes. "You don't listen to Jason Mraz?"

"Never heard of him. I'm more of a Vita's girl."

"Who's that?"

"Never mind. When can you get Stevens to the station?"

"I'll call right now. As soon as I get outside."

She punched at the buttons of her cell phone. Over her shoulder, she shouted, "Calling in the request now, Folley. Get Aaron. We'll meet at the medical examiner's."

He started down the stairs, intent on making the call to Aaron that he didn't want to make.

Chapter 10

The security camera's disc from his sister's apartment building sat in the passenger seat beside Aaron. He wondered what Folley would say now. Would the police finally get seriously involved? Now he had evidence. Now he had the kidnappers' faces on camera. Folley and his cohorts *had* to do something. Maybe the system would work for a change.

He chuckled ruefully. *That'll be the day.*

People walked hand-in-hand along the beach in front of his car. Not a care in the world. Their worst issue was getting the rent in on time or wondering if their girlfriend was cheating on them.

Life isn't fair.

As the sun dropped in the west, Toronto came alive. The clubs would fill up for the evening, then empty after midnight, and the rave parties would start, everyone enjoying themselves while their fellow Torontonians suffered. He'd lost his dojo because some asshole used his studio as training to hurt women. Because the guy Aaron beat was in a coma, Aaron had lost his freedom. As part of the bail conditions, he had to agree not to leave the Greater Toronto Area without first notifying his lawyer. Within twenty-four hours of his bail, he had been ordered to surrender his Canadian passport. It wasn't fair. It simply wasn't fair.

If the system worked, that mother and her daughter would have had a place to go, a safe place. John Ashcroft, the man in the coma, would have been arrested, and the system would have dealt with it. But instead, the shit fell on Aaron's doorstep, and it cost him his dojo, his life's dream.

His not-guilty plea followed the request to have a jury for the trial. Aaron's lawyer, Anthony Garrett, said the jury would sympathize with Aaron's plight. They'd feel sorry for the daughter and mother—some would even feel that Aaron was justified in what he did. At least that's what Anthony was going to milk the jury for. Sympathy.

Aaron turned on the car radio. Aerosmith's lead singer, Steven Tyler, sang about Janie and how she had a gun. He leaned back and closed his eyes, trying to clear his mind. Joanne was still missing. She wasn't answering her cell phone, and he was thirty minutes away from walking into the House of Lancaster to look for whatever answers he could find. He wasn't stupid. He knew there could be trouble, but he was tired of waiting to find out what was happening. It was too late to dabble. Someone at the club knew something. They had to. Maybe they have security cameras that have a story to tell.

After three songs about failed relationships and insecure people, Aaron started his car and went to put it in reverse when his cell phone rang. He grabbed the phone, hoping and praying it was his sister.

The screen read *private.*

"Hello?"

"Aaron Stevens?"

"Yeah."

"Detective Folley here."

"You got something? Is that why you're calling?"

Aaron's gaze followed a seagull as it swooped down onto the surface of Lake Ontario, snatching at something. He wished he could be that free.

"We need to talk. I need you to come down to my office."

Aaron checked the dashboard clock. He had twenty minutes to meet Daniel and whoever else Daniel had gathered to go to the strip club.

"How about tomorrow?" Aaron asked.

"Not good. I need to see you tonight. Now."

"Now?" he asked. "Why? What's so important?"

"Just get here. We'll talk when you come in."

"Are you ordering me to the police station or asking?"

"Nothing so official. I just need to talk to you. I need your statement on Gary Weeks's abduction. Something else has come up that I can't talk about on the phone."

Aaron could hear the exasperation in Folley's voice.

"What development could be so important that you can't wait until tomorrow? I don't remember your eagerness to take my statement this morning." Aaron watched the seagull as it fought with another one in midair. "Unless, of course, you've found my sister. Is that it? Have you found Joanne?"

"Look, Aaron, it does involve your sister. Come to my

office. We'll discuss it here. I'll buy you a coffee."

"You're not giving me anything, but you want me to stop what I'm doing and come running. I need more than 'we need to talk.'"

"I can't give you more on the phone."

"I've got something for you," Aaron said.

"What's that?" Folley sounded spent. Like he hadn't bargained for such resistance and was willing to let it go.

Folley would have told him if it was good news and Joanne was coming home. It had to be bad news. They've probably found her body, and Folley's the lucky dick who gets to tell him, but now that Aaron's not coming in right away, he's off the hook. For now.

"You know the guys who nabbed Gary at the airport this morning?"

"Yeah, what about them?"

"I saw them again."

"What?" Folley sounded alive now. "Really? Where?"

"On a security camera at my sister's apartment building, escorting her out the front door the night she disappeared. I've got a copy of the recording on a disc. I've got their faces on camera."

"That's great. When you're giving me your statement on what you saw this morning, you can also tell me where and how you came into possession of the recording. It'll give us something to work with. Bring it in with you."

"I'm not coming in," Aaron said, his stomach clenching at the loss of his sister. Something terrible had happened to Joanne, and now he was alone. Folley's evasiveness and refusal to tell him anything over the phone made him sure of it. He didn't want to realize this, but he had no choice.

"Joanne's been found, hasn't she?" he whispered into the phone, closing his eyes on the seagulls playing in the falling light of the sun in front of his vehicle.

He was met with silence. He waited as the tears came. The grief, unbearable and utterly paralyzing, swept over his body and imploded on his soul, making him scream on the inside at the injustice of life.

How I loved you, Joanne. You were the best sister. I'm sorry I wasn't there for you in your darkest moment, but I will be there now. I will make them pay. Nothing is going to stop me.

"Aaron?"

He heard Folley as if he was in a tunnel. He turned his cell phone off and dropped it in the seat beside him. When he opened his eyes, the world wasn't the same. It was darker, more ominous. The grief felt like a physical weight. One he couldn't shake off. Nobody cared. Nobody *really* cared. Human life was something others could take with impunity.

Everyone had roles. They were brothers, sisters, mothers, fathers, sons, and daughters. Loved ones would miss their relatives who succumbed to death early. Murderers never concerned themselves with whether or not loved ones would be left behind to grieve. It didn't matter. Whoever kidnapped his sister didn't care about Aaron or his grief. All they cared about was their motivation for abducting Joanne and doing whatever it was they did to her.

Maybe that was how the world really worked. Maybe people were supposed to just do whatever the hell they wanted and fuck the consequences. He could get used to that. Break the rules and see what happens.

But that went against everything the five disciplines of

Shotokan karate had taught him. Seek perfection of character, be faithful, endeavor to excel, respect others, and refrain from violent behavior. How could he do any of those things and live in this world?

"The ultimate aim of karate," he said out loud, "lies not in victory or defeat but in the perfection of the character of the participant."

He turned the car around and pulled out of the parking lot.

"Fuck that. The *perfection of the character* is over. I've had enough."

His cell phone rang beside him as he headed toward the House of Lancaster.

Private flashed across the screen.

"Fuck you, Folley. You did nothing. Now it's my turn." He wiped his face. "Now it's my turn."

He got on the QEW going west and floored it.

"I'm sorry, Joanne. I'm truly sorry."

Chapter 11

AARON PARKED TWO BLOCKS from the strip club on Morgan Avenue and made his way to the back of the building from a side street.

He spotted Daniel's twenty-year-old camper van and headed over to it.

As he neared, the passenger door lock clicked. Aaron swung the door open and hopped inside.

"Daniel," Aaron said, nodding at him. Alex and Benjamin Russell, two brothers who were the smartest students ever to come out of his dojo, sat in the back. He loved the relationship they had with Daniel. There were days in the dojo that he couldn't tell that Daniel wasn't just another brother, the way the three of them horsed around.

Having them here was an honor.

"Tell us what you need, Aaron," Benjamin said, "and we'll do it. Just say the word."

He looked from Alex to Benjamin and back to Daniel.

"What is it?" Daniel asked, impatient.

He knew Daniel would see the pain in his eyes. He knew he couldn't hide from these men.

"My sister, Joanne … is dead," Aaron said.

"What?" Daniel slapped the steering wheel. "I'm so sorry. How could that be?"

"What are you saying?" Benjamin asked.

Alex didn't say anything. He was the quietest of the three but also the most dangerous. He had a ninja quality in his approach to the art of karate. He sat in the back of the camper van, cracking his knuckles while he listened.

"The police called me tonight and said they needed to 'talk.'" He used air quotes to emphasize the word. "They wouldn't tell me why, just that they needed to talk. When I asked Detective Folley directly if the police had found her body, he didn't answer. It all leads back to this strip club somehow."

"How?" Daniel asked.

"I'm not entirely sure. That's why I asked you guys to come. I was here earlier today, and they kicked me out. A dancer said Joanne left here three nights ago with a rich British guy, but I have new information that the dancer probably lied." He addressed the two in the back. "Also, this British guy paid the club off to remain silent. For whatever reason, he can't have people know he was here. I have no idea what that means, but I want answers, and someone inside that building knows something. That's why you're here."

Benjamin nodded. "Go on. Tell what us we're to do."

Alex finished cracking his fingers and started in on his

neck. It was unnerving, but Aaron understood that was how Alex prepared. He had a process, and it worked for him.

"All I want to do is find the owner and get him to talk to me. I need information, that's it. But since I predict we'll have trouble with the bouncers, I need them to be put to sleep," he motioned to the pressure point on his neck, making it clear what he meant. "No one gets hurt. Let them attack first, so it's all self-defense. We're in, we're out. That's it. I will talk to the DJ and have the public escorted out first. The club will be ours for however long it takes to get answers. Then we leave, and I'll go and see what the police wanted me for and tell them what we found out. Deal?"

All three men nodded and held up scarred fists to tap in unison.

"Let's roll."

Aaron led them to the back door. He opened it and stepped inside, Daniel on his heels, Alex and Benjamin following close behind.

The first bouncer was a different one from earlier.

Aaron smiled. "I was wondering, where's the bathroom?" He lifted his hand as the large bouncer turned to point. He found the exact spot on the man's neck and jabbed with the proper pressure needed to enable a three- to five-minute sleep.

"I thought you said let them attack first," Benjamin said.

"That was for you guys, so you don't get in trouble. Don't worry about me. Now, when he wakes, put him back out. If he becomes trouble, knock him out—just no coma. I've had enough of that." He waited until Benjamin acknowledged him. "Also, don't let anyone else enter. I'll have the customers filing through that door within a few minutes. Make sure they leave."

He headed into the main part of the club with Daniel and Alex right with him. Train was singing *Soul Sister.*

How appropriate, Aaron thought.

Another bouncer sat at the bar, the one with the brass knuckles from the parking lot earlier. Before he could say a word, Alex slipped around him, jumped onto a table, spun sideways, and clipped the beefy man in the forehead with one the softest kicks Aaron could claim to have seen. It snapped the man's head back fast enough to have the brain make contact with the inside of his skull, knocking him out in less than a second. If karate could be ballet, Alex would be the prima donna.

Alex landed on his feet and shrugged at Aaron as the bouncer slipped off his bar stool.

"Sorry, he looked like trouble," Alex explained.

"Be cool," Aaron cautioned.

He stepped toward the DJ booth. A few customers saw the hit on the bouncer, but no one moved. After Alex's flying, spinning kick, Aaron didn't know many men who would try to stand up.

The dancer on stage slowed her performance, holding onto the pole. Everything in the club slowed down as Aaron's adrenaline kicked in. He was in the zone as a specialist in the art of Shotokan karate.

Near the DJ booth, he caught sight of another bouncer coming out of the bathroom at the back. With a quick finger motion, Daniel was off to add another number to the sleeping security men.

A young, tattooed man with headphones on in the DJ booth stared at Aaron.

"Turn it off," Aaron said.

The DJ shook his head. "I can't do that."

"Did you see what happened to the bouncer at the bar?"

The DJ nodded, his mouth remaining open.

"Do you want that to happen to you?"

The DJ flipped a switch on the panel in front of him. The club instantly fell into a deafening silence.

"Now, tell everyone to leave. There has been an emergency. Customers must leave within one minute, or my friends and I will start breaking bones. Do it now—"

Movement from behind, a shadow across the wall to his left, and Aaron dropped toward the floor. A beefy arm swung over his head so close he felt the breeze part his hair.

As Aaron neared the floor, he slipped his right foot out and spun in a circle, connecting with the man's ankles in a perfect foot sweep. As the fourth bouncer lost his balance, he grabbed at the door for purchase, found none, and fell hard on his ass.

Aaron lifted off the floor at the same second the bouncer landed, aiming to fly over the man. He landed just behind the bouncer's head, which he wrapped in his arms and brought him close to his chest. He locked his arms around the bouncer's neck, resting his right biceps against the man's Adam's apple. With each flex of his arm, the bouncer choked.

Aaron leaned in and whispered in the bouncer's ear. "I hate when people sneak up on me. It really pisses me off."

He looked up at the DJ. "Make the announcement for everyone to leave, or I will huff, and I will puff, and I will blow this fucking building down. Do it now."

He flexed his biceps.

***

Jackson turned into the lot of the House of Lancaster and parked in a back corner spot. Hugh hadn't eaten anything for dinner, nor had he been talkative. Jackson hated when Hugh got moody and head-fucked a problem. What Hugh didn't get was that the brother wasn't an issue. They would have plenty of time to talk to the brother as soon as they were done with the strip club. Plenty of time to *torture* the brother.

"You ready?" Jackson asked.

Hugh didn't answer or nod. He offered nothing in the way of acknowledging Jackson's presence. He just sat there, staring out the windshield.

"I guess that means you are," Jackson said.

Jackson climbed into the back of the van and started loading the MP5s they had brought along. He also grabbed three small containers of C-4.

"What the fuck is going on?" Hugh snapped.

"He talks. Holy shit," Jackson said as he checked the magazine on his sidearm.

"Look." Hugh gestured out the windshield.

Jackson crab-walked back to the driver's seat. "What the fuck *is* going on?"

People were filing out the back door of the club. One man after another, some drunk, some running for their cars, others heading out to the street, probably in search of cabs.

"What's this?" Jackson asked out loud. "Something's not right. Have they been tipped off?"

"No one knew we were coming except Clive," Hugh said. "This isn't his work. He needs casualties."

Jackson was happy Hugh was talking again, but he hated that it took something going wrong to bring his voice back.

Fucking negative idiot, he thought.

"Doesn't change a thing," Jackson added. "We blow the joint and kill whoever's inside, especially the employees. The customers were supposed to be collateral, so it's probably a good thing they're leaving."

Hugh grabbed his door and jumped out of the van.

"Hey!" Jackson shouted after him. "Where are you going?" He slipped open the side door and hopped out to stand beside Hugh. "What are you doing?"

"That fucking brother has something to do with this. That's my guess."

"How?" Jackson asked, shaking his head at the notion. "No way. He got kicked out earlier today. Why would he come back and make the customers leave? He's not psychic."

"I don't know. I can't see his car, but something tells me I'm right."

"Okay, let's go in, take care of business, and if you're right, we'll grab him and sweat him in the van."

Hugh started for the club's back door as customers filed out.

"Hey, wait. You need your gun."

"You bring it," Hugh shouted over his shoulder.

"Shit." Jackson grabbed as much ammunition as he could carry and scrambled after his partner, the MP5 machine gun held out in front of him.

Chapter 12

FOLLEY TRIED CALLING AARON half a dozen times before he finally gave up. It was Angela Wheeler's call that he regretted taking. She would finish at the crime scene soon and wanted to know when to meet Aaron. In Folley's first year of handling missing persons cases, he rarely had to make the call to inform the family of the untimely death of their missing member. Usually, homicide would take over the case, leaving Folley to look for the next missing person.

Having to deal with someone like Aaron Stevens made him feel inept. He was good as a street cop. When they offered him small roles as an undercover cop in narcotics, things had been okay. His real strength was in the investigation. He was a detail-oriented man. Just over twelve months ago, he was moved to Twelve Division to oversee missing persons cases. At that time, he still had open cases, cold cases, and a few he'd found through a solid internet search. The worst case he recalled in recent memory was the thirteen-year-old girl who had gone missing after arguing with her mother about internet usage. She was located two weeks later in a motel room with the predator who had lured her away from her safe home through a false Facebook profile.

What Folley did held value. Even if he wasn't as gung ho as he used to be in the early days, he knew what they did at Twelve Division was good. More often than not, family members were reunited, and everyone moved on.

Then, there were cases like Joanne Stevens. Missing three days, no clues, an angry brother, no parents, and a three-day headache that Folley couldn't shake. Had he been thinking clearly three days ago, he might have listened to Aaron's cell phone message that his sister had left for him the night she disappeared.

He had to face the truth. The police wouldn't even take a missing persons report until that person was missing for at least twenty-four hours. If the missing person was an adult, they usually got the family to call all known associates, ring their cell phones, stop at local watering holes, etc. The police just didn't have the manpower to hunt down every missing person in Toronto who just wanted to be left alone for a couple of days after a fight with their boyfriend or mother. There was no way they could manage that kind of load.

Calling family members to come in for positive IDs was not something any cop enjoyed, Folley the least.

He could drive to Aaron's apartment to check and see if he was home, but he was enough of a detective to know that Aaron was in his car the last time they talked, and if he didn't want to come to the police station, it was because he had something important to do, which meant he wouldn't be home.

"Where are you, Aaron Stevens, and what are you up to tonight?" Folley asked out loud.

He sat in his car outside a Starbucks, sipping a café mocha, trying to piece together the next move. Once Angela requested his transfer for him to assist homicide, he would be busy as hell for a few weeks. This was his only chance to talk to Aaron and get his full statement, something he reminded himself that he should have taken that morning when he'd had the chance. Angela had asked him to, and now he couldn't locate the man.

Why would Angela ask to transfer him? Maybe the prettiest woman in law enforcement in Toronto had the hots for him. Maybe she wanted to work closer to get to know him better. The idea pleased him, but could it be true?

He had been single far too long. Courting Angela would be a treat, sleeping with her a dream.

His phone rang, breaking his reverie.

"Hello?"

"Angela here." She was all business. "You don't have Aaron with you, do you?"

Shit! "No."

"Called him?"

"Yeah."

"Where is he? Did he say he was on his way to the station?"

"No, he …"

"I know where he is," Angela stated.

"You do?"

"Yeah. How close are you to the House of Lancaster strip

club on The Queensway? Not the one on Bloor."

"Very close. Maybe eight minutes out. Why?"

"I had one of my guys pull up everything they could on the bodies at Casa Loma. We knew that Jan and Joanne both worked at the House. So did Nancy Demeers. They all went missing on the same night, am I right?"

"No, the Demeers woman is new. I don't have a case file on her. Jan and Joanne, I did."

"Okay, whatever. They all worked together, and we just got a call that patrol cars were being sent to the House. Someone is breaking the place up."

"Breaking the place up?"

"Yeah, apparently, a waitress called from her cell phone and said three guys walked in just before nine tonight and beat up the bouncers. Some high-flying gymnastic karate shit. They're trying to get the DJ to order everyone out of the building. The DJ had the mic open, and the waitress was on with the dispatcher at 911 when someone said they would huff and puff and blow down the place if his demands weren't met. But you wanna know the best part?"

Folley started his car and set his café mocha in the coffee holder, already knowing Aaron was *breaking* the place up. The same Aaron who owned his own karate dojo. The same Aaron who just lost his sister, who worked at the House of Lancaster and wasn't coming in when the detective handling the case called him. "What's the best part?"

"The waitress said she recognized one of the guys."

Folley moved into traffic and started toward the House of Lancaster, his foot crushing the pedal. "Who is it? Aaron Stevens?"

Angela continued as if he didn't speak. "She told the

dispatcher that the same guy went to the club that morning looking for his sister, Joanne Stevens. That tells me that Aaron wants revenge. How soon before you can get there? We need this guy. We also need to know why he was at the airport this morning. My gut tells me he may have something to do with all this."

Your gut would be wrong, Angela. He's just pissed off.

"I'm less than five minutes out," Folley said, hitting the siren and the lights as he disconnected the phone.

No, Angela wasn't romantically inclined toward him. No, she had no interest. Folley felt like a fool for thinking otherwise. He was her go-to guy. Her lackey.

He slammed the pedal down harder as his anger at the thought that she would even be interested in him made him ashamed of how high school he felt.

"You're a fucking dick, Folley."

He also wondered how she made homicide, deducing Aaron as a suspect without having met him.

Unless she brought him up in the system and saw his attempted murder charge from six weeks ago.

Chapter 13

THE BOUNCER STRUGGLED, BUT Aaron held firm.

"How many customers are left?" Aaron asked.

The DJ looked through his rectangular window into the club. "No one left that I can see. Just the guys you came in with and three sleeping bouncers."

"Good," Aaron said, then leaned in close to the ear of the man he still held. "Are you going to direct me to the owner of this fine establishment, or do I have to start breaking bones?"

"The owner …" the bouncer managed and then choked. Aaron let up on his biceps. The man breathed in deeply and then continued. "The owner isn't here. He's rarely here at this hour."

"Then you can tell me what I want to know." Aaron lifted his head up and to the side. "Everything okay out there?" he shouted.

"Yeah. We're all good," Daniel called back.

Aaron reasoned that Daniel probably brought his bouncer into the main area to stay close to the rest of them after all the customers had filed out and he had locked the back door to the club.

"Tell me," Aaron said to the bouncer. "What happened three nights ago?"

"I have no idea—"

Aaron cut him off with a violent pull of his arm, and the man's air tube all but shut down. He didn't gag or choke, as air couldn't move in or out. The man's face reminded Aaron of a fish gasping on the dock. Both of the bouncer's meaty arms clung to Aaron's forearm, but in his current lock on the guy's neck, no amount of force could budge it.

"Wrong answer," Aaron said.

The DJ moved away from his music panel.

Aaron turned fast and addressed the wiry man. "Don't!"

The DJ stopped.

"Sit!" Aaron ordered through clenched teeth as he released the man's airway. The DJ dropped and sat in the corner of his little booth. The man in Aaron's arms coughed and gagged until he got his breathing back under control.

Something loud banged in the bar area.

"What was that?" Aaron yelled. He couldn't have this fall apart. He needed to stay anonymous because he knew this wouldn't go over well if his attempted murder trial jury heard about him attacking a strip club and using his obvious talents, yet again, to subdue and hurt members of the public. It would frighten the jury to have him on the street.

"Nothing," Daniel answered. "We found a waitress in the bathroom. She's cool now."

"Okay."

Aaron forced down a gag at the smell coming off the large bouncer.

Of all the customers they ordered out of the building, one of them would have called the cops by now. He figured he probably had five minutes or less. He needed answers before time ran out. "Tell me what you know. Speak now, or down you go."

"Okay, okay," the bouncer said.

"Good boy. Start talking."

The bouncer cleared his throat. "Fuck you."

"Wrong answer."

Aaron increased the pressure of his grip. The bouncer fought hard, his hands clawing at Aaron's forearm, but Aaron held firm. The bouncer was out in less than a minute, as if sleeping off a hangover. He released him and stood.

"Your turn," he said.

The DJ put up both hands in protest. "No, please don't."

"How old are you?" Aaron asked, standing over the DJ.

"Nineteen."

Aaron saw a small puddle forming under the kid.

He just pissed himself.

"Were you working three nights ago?"

The kid nodded hard and fast.

"Who was here? What happened? Did you know my sister, Joanne Stevens?"

He nodded again.

"Speak."

"A rich man with an accent came here looking for the Weeks brothers. He said he was their friend and told by Frank Weeks to enjoy the pleasures of the dancers that the Weeks brothers routinely used. Your sister," he leaned away as if expecting a smack, "and Jan Elliot was always with the Weeks brothers. Both girls were bought for the week by the rich guy. As I understand it, they agreed to a price with the owner here, and both dancers left with him. I heard they were taking them on a cruise or some shit."

"What was the rich guy's accent?"

"I think it was British."

Somewhere at the back of the club, Aaron heard another loud crash.

"What was that?" Aaron shouted, frustration in his voice. He felt like he was all nerves. The pressure of incoming police versus the need to find out what happened to his sister made him feel heady with the rush.

"Don't know," Daniel shouted back. "I'll go check it out."

Aaron stepped away from the spreading urine. "Anything else?" he asked the DJ.

The DJ shook his head.

"Think. What else can you tell me about the rich guy?"

"Nothing. He was loaded. Dropped a lot of cash and left with the two dancers. He had, like, an entourage with him. Two mean-looking guys are watching everything. That's it."

"What was he wearing?"

"Like I fucking know. You think I memorize everybody in and out of here?"

The kid has a point.

"Joanne's dead now."

The kid's eyes widened. Then they filled with tears. "You serious, man? No way. No *fucking* way."

"Very serious. And I think that British asshole did it. Be ready. The police are going to come asking questions because it's a murder investigation now and not just a missing persons case—"

The DJ's eyes moved to something behind Aaron in the doorway.

Aaron spun and dropped, his hands up, ready for anything.

He wasn't ready for the gun in the man's hand or the bullets that came out of it.

***

Jackson followed Hugh inside the back door of the House of Lancaster, gave Hugh his weapon, and stopped to set the first explosive to go off five minutes later. He figured that was enough time to deal with whoever was left inside and for him and Hugh to get out.

Then he ran to the front doors, secured them with the legs of a metal chair, slid into the bars of the handle, and set his second explosive, also for five minutes.

MP5 in hand, ready to fire on whoever challenged him, he turned down the short corridor leading to the club's main part.

Hugh had been quiet and fast. He already had three guys and a waitress on their knees, hands on their heads, lined up in front of the bar. Three large men, Jackson assumed were the bouncers, lie knocked out in different positions on the floor around the foursome. Jackson wasn't sure if they had already been knocked out or if Hugh had handled it.

Hugh motioned across the room to the DJ booth and told Jackson that he was going there and to watch the four on their knees. Jackson brought his MP5 around and aimed it at the four people who would be dead shortly. But he had to wait as Hugh wanted to surprise the men in the DJ booth. As far as he could tell, not another soul was in the strip club except for what he could discern: at least two muffled voices from the DJ booth. No music played.

Hugh silently traversed the floor, scattered with chairs and tables littered with half-empty, lonely beer bottles.

Jackson watched as Hugh walked up to the door of the DJ booth and raised his gun. Hugh's weapon began firing, but Jackson didn't see anything more. Something smashed into the side of his head so hard he lost his balance and lifted off the ground.

When he landed, the MP5 had fallen from his grip, his back ached, and he coughed like the wind had been knocked out of him. His mind raced, trying to figure out what hit him.

The smallest of the three men on the ground stood over him, smiling.

How did I not see him? I had my weapon trained on him. Who the fuck is this guy?

The little man launched off the ground and landed on Jackson hard.

All the lights of the strip club blinked out for Jackson.

***

Aaron moved on instinct and years of intense training. His mind had already taken in the whole DJ booth. He dove under the DJ desk, the only place to hide from an assault coming through the door. He slid into the wall under the desk, banging his shoulder hard. He didn't care as long as the bullets weren't hitting him.

The young DJ wasn't so lucky. Bullet after bullet cut into him, his body dancing on the floor. With the shooter preoccupied with the DJ, Aaron wondered for a brief second why the shooter just didn't bend over and shoot at him. But he dismissed the idea as self-preservation kicked in.

He did all that he could think of in the moment. He reached into the open and grabbed the leg of the DJ's office chair on wheels, which sat two feet away. He maneuvered it to aim at the door and shoved it at the man with the gun. He crawled from under the desk and dove across the floor toward the sleeping bouncer. Every second, he waited for the bullets to hit him, but none came.

When he landed on the bouncer, he grabbed the large man's arms in the strongest vice grip he could and twisted, rolling onto his back with the bouncer's heavy body rolling on top of him for protection.

He knew his next move would only be successful if he continued with his forward momentum. He thrust his foot toward the man in the door, using the bouncer's body as shelter.

The weapon silenced as the man stepped back, out of Aaron's reach.

He'd failed. He cringed and waited for the inevitable, his heart in his throat.

"Move the big man off you," the shooter said. "Or I will shoot through him and into your face."

Aaron waited for a heartbeat. He had tried. There was nothing else he could think to do. The only weapon he had was his hands. He didn't have a knife or a gun. He was out of options.

He eased the bouncer off and stared into the eyes of the

man Aaron had hit in the throat at the airport that morning. Aaron saw the same man on camera taking his sister out of her apartment building.

Anger coursed through him. The man with all the answers stood right in front of him. The man who kidnapped Joanne and probably killed her.

"Stand up," the man ordered as he gave Aaron space.

He knows I'm dangerous.

Aaron got to his feet, slowly, methodically, every muscle in his body ready to take the man out. "Why?" he asked. "Tell me. Why'd you do it?"

The man offered a crooked smile. "Vodka. Believe it or not, it's all about vodka. But you have to tell me how you knew. What brought you to the airport this morning and now here? Tell me everything before I kill you."

"One day, when you die, your life will flash before your eyes. You should've made that movie worth watching."

Before the shooter could react, something knocked him into the doorframe so hard that Aaron heard the wood crack. Aaron dropped and dove aside as the man's weapon went to fully automatic fire again.

Then it stopped as Alex drove his foot into the man's face and throat.

"Enough!" Aaron shouted. "Don't kill him."

Alex stopped instantly.

"I asked you guys here to help. I couldn't live with myself if you were up on murder charges." Aaron got to his feet and brushed himself off. "Oh, and thanks. You saved my life. I owe you."

"That's why you brought us," Alex said. "I'm here to help."

Aaron wondered how he would explain this to the police. The DJ was dead. The bouncer was now bleeding in three spots as the second round of bullets caught him in his sleep. It looked like he wouldn't be waking up again.

They had to leave and disappear.

"Come on. Let's get out of here."

He started out of the booth with Alex on his heels when an explosion rocked the building from somewhere by the back door.

"What the *fuck*?" Aaron yelled, covering his ears.

The lights flickered, and dust drifted down from the tiled ceiling.

"We have to get out of here," Aaron yelled. Two tables over, he spotted the shooter's driver from the airport. Daniel and Benjamin nodded toward Alex, who shrugged and smiled.

Alex was always the top of his class, the most dangerous.

They owed their lives to Alex, but the celebration had to be postponed.

He spied an exit sign in the far corner to his right.

"Come on," he said as the distant wail of police sirens resounded throughout the building.

Another explosion knocked them all to their knees. The lights went out. Aaron balanced on a chair and got to his feet. The battery-operated emergency lights flickered on above the exit door. There was enough light for Aaron to see that all of them were holding hands now, including the waitress from the bathroom.

I wonder if she knows anything.

He guided them to the exit door and kicked it open as police cars roared into the parking lot.

"Follow me," he shouted behind him as everyone released each other's hands.

The emergency vehicles were lining up at the front of the building on The Queensway, multicolored lights flashing across the walls of the buildings on the street. Only two cruisers had come to the back of the building so far. A fire had started by the back door where most of the customers came and went. He quickly deduced that the two men from the airport that morning had shown up with explosives, intent on removing the rest of the evidence that the British guy was ever there.

The waitress had run away, heading up the street toward the flashing lights. He motioned for his friends to follow him. Getting to Daniel's camper van was now out of the question.

He led them across the street, away from the burning strip club, toward his car a few blocks over, wondering what the hell was so special about vodka that so many people had to die.

He resolved that he would find out at all costs because Joanne deserved better.

Chapter 14

CLIVE BARON RECLINED IN his plush La-Z-Boy chair, grabbed the remote, and flipped on CNN as Jessica, his assistant, fixed him a vodka. He hadn't heard from Jackson or Hugh since he landed at Sheremetyevo International Airport in Moscow and met his driver, who took Jessica and him on the over thirty-kilometer ride to his central Moscow condo. A disposal team stood on standby to clean the plane and have it readied for whenever Clive would need it again. That meant *all* the garbage, including a drugged-up young man who happened to succumb to the barbiturates in his system. The disposal team worked for Clive personally. None of them protested the good money or life he offered them. They also didn't protest certain jobs they had to clean. It was that they would find themselves being *cleaned* one day most unusually.

Two security men met him at the door of his condo and

escorted Clive and his assistant upstairs. During the rest of the flight, his cell phone remained quiet. There was no call to his private line or encrypted line and no message from his men in Toronto that the mission was complete when he got to the Moscow condo.

Absolute silence.

He changed the TV channel and brought up the internet, where he began following the Toronto news agency's Twitter accounts. *CP24* and the *Toronto Sun* were the two he felt were most accurate, tweeting in real-time.

As he browsed the tweets to see if there was anything on the House of Lancaster explosion, Casa Loma's grisly find, or the apprehension of his men, he thought about his early departure from Canada.

Maybe he should have stayed behind to make sure everything went as planned. He had the utmost confidence in his ex-Mossad men, but with no phone call, he wondered if they had failed somehow.

Clive thought back to his early days. Hustling kids in grade school, beating others up just to take their wallets to finance a night out. He had a few run-ins with the law, but for the most part, the kids of his day didn't want a repeat beating for ratting him out.

By the time he hit seventeen, Clive had buggered and killed three different boys. After losing control of the first one and taking what he wanted by force, he learned at an early age that the broken and bleeding fifteen-year-old lying with his pants around his ankles in the alley had to remain silent about what had happened to him. There was only one way to guarantee absolute silence. Clive strangled the boy with the boy's own belt, wiped his hands off, cleaned himself up, and walked away.

Six months later, the police were still hunting the man who had raped and killed the boy in the alley. They had even interviewed the boy's friends, Clive included but suspected no one so young. It was eight months later when Clive did it again, and again, he got away with it.

On his seventeenth birthday, after his third murder, he decided that the only way to enjoy all that life had to offer him would be with money. He had watched the O.J. Simpson court case, all the while knowing that Nicole had to have been murdered by O.J. He saw how O.J. played with the glove and how his legal team created reasonable doubt. He had recently read that O.J.'s legal team was suspected of tampering with the glove somehow.

Clive learned one thing from those days: it was all about money. If Clive had enough money, he could deal with any problem.

He also knew the difference between the rich and the poor was that the rich decided to be rich. So Clive decided to go after money like a predator hunting impalas.

Soon after his rough teens, Clive moved to Moscow and entered the Moscow Institute of Finance, where he attained his Bachelor of Arts and Science. He took some of the inheritance money from his father and invested in nickel. By his mid-twenties, he was partly the owner of Siberian Nickel. In this metals giant, he flourished for eighteen years, keeping his urges under control, only murdering four male youths in the cold, snowy darkness of the Siberian winter in all that time.

He sold his interests in nickel at forty-two years of age to pursue more lucrative ventures. He maintained a large stake in one of the wealthiest banks in Russia and had investments worldwide by his mid-forties. At fifty-three, he still had stakes in steel giant Evraz and mining firm Highland Gold.

According to Forbes magazine, his net worth has been estimated at $12.7 billion, making him the eighth richest man in Russia and the sixty-fifth richest man globally.

A few years ago, he was asked to become the Deputy Prime Minister of the Economy for Russia, but he refused. He had never married and had no kids. To the outside world, he was a philanderer, flying women in from all parts of the world to enjoy. Jessica Nockler, his personal assistant, was an ex-prostitute he decided to bring on full-time after a brief six-month stint in Switzerland fifteen years ago.

No one knew about his fetish for young boys but Jessica. Only one man ever discovered that secret, and he was executed instantly.

On the TV screen, the *Toronto Sun* had a small story about the bodies found at Casa Loma, but the police weren't giving out too many details. They had another tweet about firefighters fighting a blaze at a strip club in Etobicoke, but again, he couldn't find out what was happening, and none of his phones were ringing.

At least it sounds like Jackson and Hugh got the fire going.

Jessica carried a glass of vodka, neat, into his large office.

"I want you to call Jackson and Hugh's cell phones," he said. "Report to me the minute you reach either one."

"Yes, sir," Jessica said and walked out the door.

He flipped the TV back to international news and let his mind wander as he sipped his beverage. The vodka reminded him of his beginnings. Since Russia was the birthplace of vodka and they were the largest spirits consumers in the world, it was a great country in which to sell vodka.

Three years ago, he was determined to become the biggest vodka importer in Russia. He even came up with his own brand: *Absolutely Russian Vodka*. He planned to out-seat Lars Olsson Smith, whose vodka became known as *Absolut* and who had been named the King of Vodka. Clive's famous claim is to have the clearest vodka on the planet, which is seen as purer and healthier.

His rival, Roust Incorporated, is one of Russia's largest premium spirits importers. In the new year, Clive would claim to have outdone Roust. He had recently purchased an American distillery of grain alcohol from where he imported all his *Absolutely Russian Vodka* grain alcohol base directly to Russia. Because it was one of his own companies, he raised the profits to large margins at his American facility.

Russian import duties on alcohol had increased to enormous amounts. Clive directed his small team of scientists to solve this problem, which they did.

The secret they came up with would make Clive the richest man in all of Russia, a secret so valuable that Clive could never have anyone discover what he was doing. Clive would kill for that secret Frank and Gary Weeks discovered at the Toronto Island Airport after stealing one of Clive's pieces of luggage. It was the secret that cost them their lives and everyone known to them whom they may have been in contact with in the short time they held his luggage.

For Clive, the cost of silence was always death. What did Clive care about a few dead Canadians? Disposing of one dead body randomly was something Clive had become an expert on. Killing dozens in Toronto needed the right kind of person or people.

The plan was ingenious. Everything was working perfectly until that brother showed up in Toronto.

And now Jackson and Hugh hadn't reported in.

Clive's secret had to be protected at all costs, or he would be crucified, not by the legal system alone but by the common people.

He had to get more proactive. He needed someone on the case who would know what to do. He needed Nick Sturnam on board, even though Nick would charge exorbitant costs. It was time to make the call.

He set the remote control on the table beside him as Jessica knocked lightly and entered. "Nothing from Jackson or Hugh. Also, I can't find out if they've been arrested or their current status, but I'll keep checking."

"Get Nick Sturnam on the line."

"Nick?" She sounded surprised. "Are you sure?"

Clive looked her up and down and closed his eyes to remain calm. He wasn't used to many people questioning him. "Of course, I'm fucking sure. Don't ever ask me that again."

"Yes, sir."

"Get Nick on the line. Do it now. Buzz it through to this phone. Don't come in here again. Do not disturb me unless you hear from Jackson or Hugh."

"Yes, sir," Jessica said as she backed out the door, shutting it softly.

Chapter 15

Detective Folley could see the flames from six blocks back. As he drove up, red lights of emergency vehicles flashed in front of the House of Lancaster. He flipped his single dash light off and killed his siren. The area was already roped off with at least a hundred members of the public standing, watching.

The four lanes of The Queensway were backed up, and an officer directed cars getting through on one lane.

Folley parked as close as he could grabbed his cell phone and ran toward the burning building.

Aaron, what have you done now?

He knew the man had to be grieving, but this was no way to handle it. Folley would be forced to press charges if what dispatch heard from the waitress inside the club was true. With Aaron's attempted murder charge over his head, he was about to be in a lot of trouble.

Folley showed his ID and got through the taped-off area. He headed for the back of the building, where the fire was under control. Inside the cordoned-off area, police officers talked to a group of people.

Two men sat in the back of two different police cruisers parked side by side. He knocked on the back window. After he got the man's attention and confirmed it wasn't Aaron, he knocked on the other cruiser's window.

"Hey," a cop shouted as he approached Folley. "Who are you?"

Folley lifted his ID. "Detective Folley. I'm here on behalf of Detective Angela Wheeler at Homicide. I'm sure she'll be along shortly. And you are?"

"Officer Hanley. I'm in charge here until Homicide arrives. The coroner is already here." Hanley pointed. "When homicide arrives, tell them we have a stiff in the DJ booth."

"The DJ booth?"

"Yeah, it looks like these two guys," he pointed at the men in the separate cruisers, "came in with MP5 machine guns and C-4 to raze the place. When we found that one," he pointed at the cruiser on the left, "he still had another explosive on his person." Hanley gestured toward a white van parked in the back corner. "It appears that's their vehicle. It has enough weapons in the back to start a war with a small country. These two were on some kind of private mission or something. Maybe one of the dancers wouldn't let them finger her."

I'm sure it's not that simple, asshole.

Folley tried to wrap his head around everything. He thought Aaron Stevens had been here. That's what Angela had said the dispatcher recorded. How did that fit with what

Officer Hanley just said?

"And you want to know what the best part is?" Hanley asked.

Folley nodded. He could tell Hanley was eager to tell.

"These guys come with no ID, and their van is stolen. They have tats, though. It looks like ex-military tats, but I'm not the expert. When we get them downtown, we'll have a terrible time figuring out who they are because they don't have any fingerprints either, and they're not talking."

"No fingerprints?" Folley asked, aghast. "How's that? Did they burn them off?"

"Must've been some kind of acid. Who knows," Hanley said, exaggeratedly shaking his head, evidently very happy to have made the collar. As far as Hanley was concerned, he had just made the arrest of his career.

"Those people there," Folley pointed at the ten people gathered around three officers taking notes, "who are they?"

"Witnesses. They have some story about four guys coming into the club and saving everybody five minutes before these two showed up and started shooting."

"Saving everybody?" *What the fuck?*

"Yeah. The one waitress said she saw the whole thing. She said she was the one who called us. At first, the foursome looked like they were the aggressors, she said, knocking out the bouncers with some kind of high-flying kicks, but then the one guy, who she called Aaron, a brother of one of the dancers, got the DJ to have everyone exit the building. Then these two came in and took the waitress and three guys hostage while the other one opened fire on the DJ and this Aaron guy. I don't know how the tables turned, but they did, and these two were knocked unconscious. That's how we found them. The bouncers were all knocked out, too. We thought maybe they'd used gas on them or something, but they hadn't. The waitress was fine."

"Where's the four guys who saved the day?"

Hanley shrugged. "No idea. We looked for them, but they were gone. In the wind."

Folley figured the two men in the back of the cruisers were the same two who took Gary in a white van, and he guessed the van would have evidence to prove that. If these two were the same men who took Joanne Stevens, then the Casa Loma murders would be wrapped up pretty fast, which would go a long way to dispel public fear that a mass murderer or serial killer was on the loose. But how did Aaron fit into all this? If he really did save the day, then where was he? Why run?

"Who owns the remaining six vehicles in the lot?"

"No idea."

"Run the plates. Find out if they belong to the four men who ordered everyone out of the club. While you're doing that, I want to talk to those witnesses, especially the waitress. When Detective Wheeler gets here, she'll be taking over the case. I'm pretty confident this is connected to the Casa Loma murders found earlier tonight. In the meantime, get me the names and addresses of the owners of these cars."

"Got it."

Folley walked over and asked the waitress to come talk to him.

Her eyes were bloodshot, and the makeup streaked down her cheeks from crying. She stood beside him, fumbled with a half-smoked cigarette, and lit the tip, her hand shaking as what she had just been through worked its way through her system.

"You doing okay?" Folley asked.

She looked at him sideways. "What do you care?"

"Having those guys point their weapons at you had to be difficult."

She took two long puffs on her cigarette, blew the smoke out, and then stomped on the butt, squishing it under her shoe. "I just can't take anymore. I'm quitting this place. I tried to stop smoking two years ago, but working here got me smoking again. I'm fucking done. I want out."

"That, I can understand," Folley said, trying his best to sound consoling, a friend. "Can you tell me what happened here tonight?"

"I already told the cops what happened."

"Yeah, but I need to hear it from you myself. Is right here, right now, good for you?" he asked in his most understanding voice. "Or would you rather go downtown to the station where I can take a formal statement?"

"You wanna know the truth, the whole truth, and nothing but the truth?"

"Something like that."

"I'm pretty freakin' scared." She hunched her shoulders and lowered her head, about to cry. "Aaron, Joanne's brother, came by earlier looking for his missing sister. I was wrong about him. He's one of the good guys, but I thought Aaron was the bad guy when he flipped the bouncer and twisted his finger almost off this morning."

Folley gestured for her to keep going.

"He came tonight and said he was gonna blow the place up, but then those two came back in, and they had guns—"

"What do you mean, 'came back in'?" Folley asked.

"You *know* them?"

She glanced at the cruisers, then up at the night sky. "Yeah. But I'm not saying anything else."

"Why not?" Folley asked.

"Because of them."

"I don't understand. Explain it to me."

The waitress straightened her hair, pulled it back, and then pushed it behind each ear. She scanned the ground, appearing to want her cigarette back, but it wasn't coming back from its squished existence. "I don't want to talk about it."

"Why not?"

"Because of what happened here tonight."

"You're talking in circles."

She looked him in the eye. "I will tell you what I saw here tonight. I won't hide anything. But I can't talk about nothing else that deals with them."

"I'm still not following."

She looked away and put her back to the cruisers with the two suspects. "You're pretty stupid for a detective."

He didn't rise to her insult. He waited, knowing she wanted to tell him something and that he could take her to the station and sweat her for information.

"Those two men showed up here tonight to kill everybody," she said.

"That part seems clear."

"That means they came to kill me, too. Because of what happened three nights ago." She stopped and fiddled with her hair, twisting it around a finger. "Which is something I won't talk about."

"Maybe by telling me what happened, I can help. If I

know the whole story, I can ensure those two go away for a long time."

"Trust me, it's not that simple."

"I hear you, but I don't understand you. Have it make sense for me."

"Something happened three nights ago. The bouncers and I were witnesses. Don't you see? If I talk, I'm dead."

"If they came to kill you tonight, you have to consider something. The people who hired them will send others."

The waitress's hair fell in front of her face, and she left it there. Some of the other witnesses were dispersing as the officers moved away. Things were calming down, the tension leaving the air. But the nightmare was still very real for the waitress in front of him. She wiped at her eyes.

"I probably should've asked you first, but what's your name?"

"Julie Kingsley. I've only been working here for two months, and I quit. Don't come here looking for me."

"I'm going to need your phone number and address," Folley said as he pulled out a small pad and pen.

Julie gave him her information and even her date of birth when he asked for it.

"Last question. Where is Aaron now?"

"No idea. How should I know?" Julie wiped her face and pushed her hair back over her ears.

"Did you see him leave?"

"I was so scared, I ran for the front of the building where the police were showing up. I think they went down the street that way," Julie said, nodding at the road in the back of the club.

"They? You mean the foursome?"

"Yeah. The guys who saved our lives."

"Detective Folley," Hanley said as he ran up.

"Yeah, what is it, Hanley?"

"Detective Wheeler is entering the building at the front and wants to see you up there."

"Okay, thanks. I'll head over. Can you take Julie here and place her in an empty cruiser?"

"What?" Julie snapped.

"I'm going to need to talk to you again," he told her. "We'll do it at the station where those two can't watch you talk. I need to know everything about what happened three nights ago."

"I'm not comfortable with this. I don't even know if I'm ready to talk about it. It's late. Can you let me think about it?"

"Whoever sent those two to raze this place and kill everyone in it, with as much weaponry as they had, won't be waiting until tomorrow. Hanley, that goes with all the bouncers, too. Everyone must be taken into custody until we know more about what's happening here."

"Got it," Hanley said and headed off.

"Listen, Julie. I have something to tell you. What I'm about to tell you hasn't leaked to the media yet, but it will by tomorrow. Jan Elliot and Joanne Stevens are dead, as well as Nancy Demeers. All their bodies were found tonight, with Frank and Gary Weeks's bodies, too. This is very serious. These guys don't play games. You were supposed to be on the list as well as everyone in this club tonight."

Julie covered her mouth with her hand and slid down the wall to crouch on her knees. Her eyes widened in shock, and tears dripped as her shoulders hitched up and down.

"I need to know everything you know to stop the people who did this. Having you downtown at the station will offer you protection until we figure out what's happening."

Her nod was barely evident, but he caught it. Hanley returned and gestured to Julie. Folley nodded, and Hanley helped her to her feet and started walking her to an empty cruiser.

Before Folley met Angela, he gazed down the dark street where Julie had said Aaron ran.

Aaron, where are you, and what are you doing now?

Chapter 16

AARON WAS FIGHTING THE biggest internal battle he had ever encountered. Should he run or turn himself in? He could grab money and food and drive the hour and a half south to cross the Peace Bridge in Niagara Falls and get lost in the States somewhere. Or he could drive to Folley's office and tell him everything he knew. Would Folley lock him up for attacking the bouncers? Or would Aaron look like a hero for getting all the paying customers out before the gunmen showed up? His friends were only there to help if things went bad, and it did. What would happen to them?

He had taken the three of them to Daniel's house for the night and left, telling them he had to take the recording of the two men escorting his sister out of her building to the police station. The same two men from the strip club. But he hadn't yet because he still wasn't sure if he could.

He had slept by a beach in Oshawa—almost an hour's

drive out of Toronto where no one would expect to find him —with the front seat reclined as far as it would go.

The early morning ride into Toronto had been horrible as he sat in the bumper-to-bumper traffic at seven-thirty that morning. It was after nine in the morning, and he was parked in Twelve Division's lot, still debating the right move as the morning sun beat in through his passenger side window.

The fact that he was in the police station's parking lot told him he had made up his mind, but he still wasn't sure.

The system had failed too often in the past. Could he trust them now, when he needed them the most? Folley had tried Aaron's cell phone numerous times throughout the night, no doubt wanting to know where he was.

There had been witnesses who had seen the whole thing last night. The waitress could verify Aaron's side of the story. If only he didn't have the attempted murder charge over his head, the cops wouldn't look at him like *he* was a criminal. They didn't know who he was. They would judge him by his actions, and that was it. Whether he was found guilty or not, he had a criminal charge over his head, and that's how the system treated him.

"Screw it." He started the car. "I'm outta here. They can solve whatever case they have to solve without me. They're the fucking cops. It's their job."

He put the Nissan in drive and then stopped.

The main doors to the police station opened, and the waitress from the strip club walked out onto the concrete steps. Behind her, a police officer exited the building and walked her toward a police cruiser.

They must have taken her statement and were going to drive her home. He wondered what she had told them. Did she bash Aaron and his friends, or did she remember that Alex had taken out both shooters and saved everyone's life?

Aaron wanted to know what she told the cops before he approached them. She was his chance to find out what was happening on the inside.

The officer opened the front door of the cruiser for her, waited until she got in, and then closed it. After getting in himself, he reversed out of his spot and started for the exit.

Aaron pulled out of his parking space slowly, waited until the cop car turned left onto Dixie, and then drove to the exit. He followed as closely as he could for over ten blocks until he lost the cruiser to a red light. He waited and watched the police car in the distance, but the light didn't change. With the police car almost lost to sight, Aaron had no choice. With a break in traffic, he gunned the Nissan's engine, racing through the intersection. He nearly clipped the back of a pickup, the guy laying on the horn as he sped by. He accelerated his car to fifteen over the limit to catch up to the cruiser that had disappeared around a corner up ahead.

He couldn't lose them. He had no idea where she lived.

Aaron scanned the cars ahead of him.

Nothing.

"Shit," he said as he smacked the steering wheel.

He slowed the Nissan back to the speed of the traffic around him. The summer sun beat down through the window. He flicked on the air conditioner and wondered what he would do next. As far as he was concerned, he couldn't do anything right. Last night's fight at the strip club was dangerous and stupid. He had a machine gun fired at him. He almost got killed and saw the DJ die. An innocent man torn apart by bullets meant for Aaron. He had never seen a man die before. The closest Aaron had been to death was John Ashcroft, the man Aaron had put in a coma at his dojo. Aaron was so pumped up on adrenaline last night, trying to stay alive, that he hadn't considered the consequences of running from the scene of a murder.

Why did those men come in so heavy with such firepower? How did vodka fit into all of it?

He was in a serious amount of trouble. The only option was to drive back to the police station and try to make things right. He couldn't live on the run. He wasn't that kind of guy. He didn't know the first thing about obtaining a fake ID, living under a false name, and assuming a new identity. It was better to face the music, get it over with, and then go on living.

But what about my sister? Does she get to keep on living?

The light ahead turned red at Hurontario Street. He considered running the red for a brief moment. Maybe a huge dump truck would take him out, and all the pain would end right then and there.

He stopped at the light and checked his rearview mirror.

Sitting directly behind him was the police car he had been searching for. The waitress sat in the passenger seat, staring out the side window, appearing uninterested in what the cop was saying. The cop stared straight ahead at Aaron's Nissan, his mouth moving.

What the hell happened? Did they stop for gas? Or is the cop tailing me now?

The cop moved in his seat. The police car's horn sounded, and Aaron jumped. The light was green, and the cars around him were already moving through the intersection.

Aaron eased forward and got up to the speed limit while glancing in his mirror as often as he could without swerving. His speed stayed slow, making other cars go around him. He kept it that way, hoping the cruiser would follow suit and pass him.

He assured himself that the cop held no interest in him. It had been a simple delay of some kind. They must have stopped off for gas or to buy a drink.

Another traffic light turned yellow. Aaron gently applied the brakes and stopped as the light turned red. The cruiser moved out from behind him and pulled up alongside. Aaron fiddled with the dials on his car radio so neither occupant of the police cruiser could see him. He looked at the traffic light and back to the radio, the air conditioner vent blowing cold air directly into his face.

The light changed to green. As he pulled forward, he snuck a quick glance at the cop car and saw the waitress staring out the window. She wasn't looking at him. He saw bags under her eyes and the bloodshot sclera that said she had had a rough night. They all had a rough night after living through the fear of two men with machine guns coming to kill everyone. She must have been through an extra tough evening as she probably spent the whole night telling cop after cop what had happened in the club.

He fell in behind the cruiser and let a little distance open up between them so as not to be noticed, but not enough distance that he would lose them again.

The cruiser entered the Queensway block near Royal York Road and turned right, heading north. Aaron sped up to the intersection and turned right fast, almost hitting the cruiser that had parked on the side of the road, his four-ways flashing.

Aaron tapped his brakes and swung the wheel hard to the left to miss the stopped car without checking his blind spot. Luckily, no vehicles were coming, and the driver in the police cruiser didn't look his way as Aaron drove by.

He watched in his mirrors as the waitress got out of the car. The police cruiser performed a U-turn and drove south on Royal York Road.

Aaron turned into a driveway about ten houses up and waited for the waitress to approach him. He had no idea what he would say first, nor did he know if she would freak out at the sight of him, but he needed to talk to her. She had to know something about the night Joanne was taken. Aaron assumed that was the reason the two thugs had shown up at the club—to destroy all the evidence, even witnesses.

Three houses short of where Aaron waited, she turned up a driveway, but not before looking in all directions to see if anyone followed her. She lingered on Aaron's idling Nissan momentarily and then walked behind a white house with an empty driveway.

Aaron headed north one block and parked on a side street.

He wondered how many laws he was breaking. Following a police officer had to be against the law somehow. Usually, it was the other way around. Stalking the waitress to her home with the intent of questioning her about something that happened almost four days ago had to be a form of harassment.

He dismissed all the negative thoughts, thinking only about his sister and knowing she had been killed. He turned off the Nissan and got out. He slipped the Kubaton on his keychain along the inside edge of his pocket so the keys could remain exposed. He needed it easy to grab in case of trouble. Lately, that's all that came his way.

He started along the backs of the houses that fronted onto Royal York Road one block over. If there was a way to enter from the back, he wanted to find it. Coming in from the front left him too exposed.

Lining himself up with the white house the waitress had entered, there was a house with yellow siding and bars over the windows in the basement. The yellow house had a backyard that appeared to be a large cage. Signs told intruders to beware of dogs. In the few seconds he stood in front of the yellow house, he heard three barks, two of them from different dogs.

I guess I'm not going in this way.

He walked back around the block and up to the front of her house. What was he going to say? He had no idea what she had discussed with the police, nor did he know what they had told her about him. Would Folley, or any other officer, tell her about the criminal charges pending against him? If they had, the waitress would have been quite scared if he had simply walked up and knocked.

But what else could he do? He didn't know how to break into a home. Adding more criminal charges to his resume wasn't in the plans. Talking to the waitress and leaving was all he wanted.

The front door of the house opened. Aaron hesitated on the first few steps of her walkway as she held the door.

"I was about to make a cup of tea," she said. "Care to join me? Or will you stand out in front of my house until one of my neighbors calls the police? I assure you, I've had enough with the cops to last a lifetime."

She went in, the screen door shutting behind her, and the inside door left ajar.

She had seen him in the Nissan. She wouldn't have issued an open-door invitation if she thought he was a threat.

Aaron shut and locked the door behind him.

Chapter 17

JESSICA KNOCKED ON CLIVE'S door as he was about to fall asleep in his chair.

"Come," Clive called, rubbing his eyes. He lowered the chair and dropped his feet to the ground to sit up.

The door opened a foot, and Jessica stuck her head in. "Sorry to bother you, but I have Nick on encrypted line four."

Clive waved her away and grabbed the phone.

"Nick?"

"I'm listening."

"Are you still in the Toronto area?"

"How is that important?"

"Something went wrong in Toronto four days ago, and I need it cleaned up."

"Send your ex-Mossad dogs in."

"I did."

Nick stayed silent. It always infuriated Clive to listen to

someone breathing on the other end of the phone. Nick was the only one he allowed to do it.

"My Mossad team may have failed. I need your services."

Clive waited, but Nick still didn't respond.

"You there?" Clive asked.

"Yes. Explain what you need?"

"Witnesses need accidents. Jackson and Hugh may have to go, also." Clive was sure he heard the subtle intake of breath as Nick heard that Clive's two pets were to be euthanized. "I'm serious. The Toronto job was important, and they haven't checked in. My guess is they've been arrested, but I haven't been able to find out yet. Is this something you can handle?"

"I'll call you back. Give me five minutes."

The line went dead. Earlier, when Clive had waited for Jessica to get Nick on the line, he had called his contact at the RCMP in Ontario to see if he could get anything on Jackson and Hugh, but he hadn't heard back from him yet.

Over the years, Clive had built up contacts with the FBI, the CIA, Interpol, MI6, the RCMP in Canada, France's Police Nationale, the Mossad, and even Belgium's Police Fédérale. Several times, he had avoided arrest due to a well-placed call at the right time. In his business, the business of wealth and making it at all costs, he needed allies. He knew Interpol and the FBI were tracking his whereabouts, a few hotshot agents gunning for him, but they never got enough to press charges. At least not charges that would stick.

Clive stayed under the radar, getting his mercenaries to do the work for him. He remained elusive because whenever someone like the Weeks brothers learned something damaging about him, Clive was decisively responsive, removing whoever was in his way. He had learned young that dead mouths don't talk.

He eased his considerable bulk out of the chair and walked to the liquor cabinet. Uncapping a bottle of Scotch, he poured himself two fingers.

Everything would be fine now. Nick Sturnam was the consummate professional. He wasn't just good at what he did. He was the best. He was also the most expensive. Otherwise, Clive would use him more regularly. Clive was rich because he wasn't stupid with his money.

Nick had proven himself worthy over the years. Even the mafia, the Cosa Nostra, had used him for a few jobs. At least, that was what Clive had gathered through his information channels a few years back when he was first introduced to Nick.

Clive sipped his Scotch. The silent TV displayed images, but he had muted it before dozing off.

The phone rang. He sat in his chair, saw line four again, and picked it up.

"I'm here," Clive said.

"Your boys are being detained. I've been told they aren't talking, and no one can figure out who they are."

Clive felt his stomach drop. If either one of the ex-Mossad mercenaries struck a deal and flipped, he would be finished. They knew too much.

"Both must be silenced immediately," Clive said.

"They're in the police station in a cell."

"I don't care if they're at the space station. They have to be silenced and fast."

"That's going to cost you."

"I know it will, but I need you to do it. Also, all the staff at the House of Lancaster must be taken care of, too."

"All the staff? The dancers too?"

"No, only the bouncers and the waitresses."

"That's a tall order."

"That's why I called you," Clive said as he shot back the rest of the whiskey. "I will have Jessica send you an email with the list of names and addresses of the staff. Find them all and close this chapter for me. Name your price?"

"That depends on how many people we're talking."

"I don't know right now, but it could be at least six, maybe eight."

"Wire me half a million deposit, and I'll get started. We'll talk money when I have your Mossad boys. They may be trouble."

Clive leaned his head back and stared at the ceiling. His stupid mistake of letting Frank Weeks steal his luggage will now cost him two of his men and at least a million dollars in cleanup.

"Just do it. Leave the second you get Jessica's email. Go to the nearest employee's house from where you are and start down the list. I want it all done within twenty-four hours or faster."

"I won't start until I see half a million wired to me. Send the email. I'll receive it on my cell phone as I'm driving. Each body will get a photo for confirmation, which I will email back to you. I'm going to my car now. Send what you have, and I will watch for the money."

Clive held the phone to his ear, but Nick had already hung up.

"Jessica," he shouted, tossing the phone to one side.

The door opened, and she stepped in.

"Email Nick everything on the staff at the strip club. He will need their full names and home addresses. Also, wire him five hundred thousand dollars immediately. I'm going to take a small nap, but I want to be up by four in the morning. When I wake, have someone here for me. I'd prefer more boyish looks this time. Be discreet. You know what to do. Go now."

The door shut, and Clive reclined in his chair, shutting his eyes, a smile on his lips.

His Toronto troubles were about to be a memory. Soon, everyone involved in the fuck-up would be dead, and his secret would remain just that—a secret.

Chapter 18

DETECTIVE FOLLEY RUBBED HIS eyes and groaned. He and Angela Wheeler had stayed up all night grilling the witnesses. A sketch artist had been called in to draw the face of the rich British man the bouncers and the waitress had told them about four nights ago.

One of the detectives recognized the sketch and, using Google Images, brought up a British man who lived in Moscow on a computer screen. Each bouncer, in succession, agreed that the man on the screen was the same man who had entered the House of Lancaster four nights ago and left with Joanne Stevens and Jan Elliot. Folley also discovered that the two men in holding cells downstairs, whom no one could identify, were with the British guy that night.

The man was identified as Clive Baron, who appeared to be hard to track down. Angela Wheeler had ordered a full search on the man's background. She wanted to know everything she could about him. It wasn't long before his name popped up in connection with human trafficking, money laundering, and murder.

According to information readily available on the internet, he owned the largest yacht in the world, *Divercity*, which was 560 feet long. It cost him over three hundred million dollars. He owned homes in many cities and traveled around the globe on his private 767 jet. Baron had never married and had no kids.

Spanish authorities once named Clive Baron in a money laundering case, which was handed off to the Russians for further investigation. As far as Angela and Detective Folley could find out, nothing more had been done about that case.

Other than rumors and assumptions, Baron appeared squeaky clean. Too clean. Whatever he was up to, it looked like Folley and Angela wouldn't be getting too close to him anytime soon.

"So what happened?" Folley asked. He grabbed a pencil and started tapping it against the wooden top of his desk. "What do you *think* happened? The two men in the holding cell, why did they try to kill everyone at the club after being seen with Baron? Or maybe that was the point."

Angela leaned against Folley's office door. "I have no idea what's going on. I do know that this case just got a hell of a lot bigger. This is going to have to be shuffled upstairs. Whatever the reason those two thugs downstairs had to destroy that club is beyond me. Nothing is making sense. In all my years in homicide, I haven't seen anything like this. There has to be a reason to kill this many people in such a short time frame."

"Unless they're terrorists. Maybe we should call the FBI

in on this. Get their take. Maybe the Americans have a file on those two downstairs."

"I don't want to do that just yet." Angela's face was stoic. "Isn't there another angle? I've got a lot of dead bodies on my hands and little evidence, but the case just wrapped up if we can determine those two downstairs did all of it."

Folley dropped the pencil and picked up the Rubik's Cube on his desk. He leaned back in his chair and spun the colors out of order. He hated that Aaron had bested him so easily. "I want to look into this case a bit more. I want to know who's pulling the trigger. If Baron was just here in Toronto, did he personally kill any of the people found at Casa Loma? If he did, we can file the arrest warrant and send it to Russia, where we can request him extradited."

Angela pushed off the door and faced him. "We've got the murderers downstairs in the holding cells. Aaron said he had footage of those two taking his sister, and he saw them at the airport the morning Gary Weeks was taken. They were found unconscious with C-4 on them and the guns that were fired inside the club. The DJ is dead. We've got first-degree murder. It was planned and executed with the explosives placed strategically. Who's to say Baron has anything to do with it? Going after him makes this case way too big. The kind of big that means we lose the collar."

"I think Baron has everything to do with this." Folley dropped the Rubik's Cube and picked his pencil up again. He hoped Angela wouldn't notice him fidgeting.

"On what grounds?"

"My hunch is those two guys work for Mr. Baron, and they're here cleaning up for him."

Angela dismissed him with a wave as she leaned on the

door. "You watch too many Jason Statham movies. People are people. They kill in fits of rage, and they kill because they're sick in the head. Sure, there are professional killers, but you're talking about hired guns, not Clive Baron. Do you really think someone as rich as Clive would need to travel around the globe in his private jet, murdering people in various countries? With that much money, he could relax for the rest of his life."

Folley stood from behind his desk. "Angela, you're tired. You're not thinking this through. Those two downstairs aren't going anywhere. We'll meet up later this afternoon or tonight and process those two, even if we don't have their names. We'll find out who they are after sending out their pictures to every major police station in Europe. My guess is we will ID them once we contact Moscow or London. Although, the one guy looks Jewish, so maybe they're Israeli, who knows." He paused to drop the pencil back into its holder. "Get some sleep. I will, too. Then we'll see what Moscow has to say about Clive Baron. It'll be morning for them when we come back tonight."

"What about Aaron Stevens? I still need his statement." She paused, lost in thought, until her eyes focused on him again. "If what you say is true, Aaron may be in danger. We sent the waitress home. What if she's in danger, too? This might not be over. We have to consider that."

"True, but I think the perps are downstairs cooling their heels. No one's going after anybody else."

"If this is as big as it looks, you can't be sure," Angela said.

"You're right, I can't. But we don't have the manpower to protect everybody who worked at the strip club."

"If Clive Baron is involved, we need to find a motive. I mean, what makes him kill like this? If it's enough to expose himself this much, it must be seriously important to him."

"True, but remember, if those two downstairs weren't interrupted by Aaron and his friends, no one would have been able to describe Clive to our sketch artist. Therefore, Clive felt he was home free." Folley approached Angela. "Go home. Get some sleep. Let's meet back here later."

As Angela left, her long hair cascaded past her shoulders in lazy curls. It was like she had come from the hairdressers even though she had just pulled an eighteen-hour shift. Her shoes clicked on the tile floor as she walked down the hall.

Folley shut his office door, then sat and leaned back in his chair, wondering where Aaron was. The license plates on the vehicles in the strip club's parking lot had come back. It looked like there was a connection between Aaron and the camper van, which was registered to Daniel Smith, a known associate of Aaron's from his old karate gym. Two uniforms had gone over to Daniel's house but had failed to locate him yet.

So far, after hearing the witness statements, Aaron has had three friends with him, and they saved everybody and then ran off. Getting Aaron's statement would help clarify why Aaron was there in the first place. He had to have had prior knowledge of the strip club attack because he showed up just in time, ordered everyone out of the building, and said something about the place blowing up. The 911 recording was clear enough to pick up his words but not clear enough to hear the entire sentence.

The cops needed to know whatever it was that tipped Aaron off. Maybe Aaron knew how Baron was involved.

Which would mean Aaron's life was still in danger.

Chapter 19

IN FRONT OF AARON, family pictures adorned the hallway walls in the waitress's home. The living room was to his left, and a parlor with a billiard table was to his right.

And here I thought the strippers made all the money. For a waitress, she sure has enough stuff.

"You take cream in tea?" she hollered from up ahead. "Or do you want coffee?"

"Cream works," Aaron shouted back.

"In what?"

For a moment, he missed what she meant. "Oh, in tea."

He followed the hall to a large kitchen with a large chandelier over a cherry oak kitchen table.

"Wow, this is some place. It's so nice."

She stood by the counter, dipping tea bags in the cups. "You sound surprised."

"Well, it's just, I don't mean anything by it, but …"

"You don't think I make enough money to afford it."

"Well, no, what I mean is—"

"It's okay," she said, stirring cream into the teacups. "This is my parents' house. I moved back in after my marriage fell apart a year ago. They're on vacation in Hawaii right now."

"Oh, nice place to go," Aaron said, hoping they'd discuss something else.

She extended a cup of tea to him. "I'm sorry about your sister."

He took the proffered tea and half smiled, not ready to talk about Joanne quite yet.

"My name's Julie. You're Aaron." She stuck her hand out, and he shook it. "Sorry about being a bitch to you yesterday. That's what I was told to do."

"Told? By who?"

Aaron sipped his tea. Peppermint wafted up his nostrils as the hot water burned his tongue.

"Come, we'll sit in the living room. I'll tell you everything I know. Maybe you'll get some closure."

Aaron sat on the loveseat, which backed up to the wall to give him an ample view of the house, the front window, and the door.

Julie sat in the chair to his right and placed her cup on a coaster atop the coffee table. Aaron did the same.

"I'm really scared," she said.

Aaron nodded. He was scared, too, but lost on what to do next. He hadn't admitted it to himself, but he was *seriously* scared. He was almost shot last night.

"I think those men wanted to kill everyone because of what Frank said."

"Frank? You mean Frank Weeks?"

Julie nodded and reached for her tea, her hand shaking.

"My sister called me and left a message the night she disappeared," Aaron started. "The message was unclear, but I heard the name Weeks, and I heard vodka, something about a ferry, and David Hornell. She said she was scared and that someone was coming after her. I later put together that David Hornell was the ferry that took people to the Toronto Island Airport. I discovered that Weeks referred to the brothers who worked at the airport. The vodka angle isn't clear yet, but last night's shooter said, 'It was all about vodka.' Does any of that coincide with what you know?"

"All of it." Julie sipped her tea again. "The day before the British guy showed up, Frank came to the club like always. Except this time, he seemed high or something, very happy and jumping all around. What was unusual was he had endless lap dances with …" She paused. "I'm sorry."

"It's okay. Just tell me. I know what my sister did."

"Well, Frank kept having dance after dance. One of the bouncers asked Joanne if everything was okay because the girls had to dance on stage, too. They had to take their turn, but Joanne stayed with Frank. I served him that night."

She set her teacup down and leaned back in her chair. She collected herself, adjusted her pants, moved her hair from her shoulders, and started again.

"Frank confided in Joanne. After midnight, she told one of the bouncers and me that Frank had stolen luggage at the airport. He said no one would ever know it was him. I think what got everyone killed was what was in that suitcase."

"What was in the suitcase?" Aaron asked.

"Apparently, there had been thousands of dollars in cash

and some sort of documents that belonged to an alcohol distillery or something."

"That's the vodka connection. It has to be."

Julie nodded. "Sounds like it. But what I don't understand is no one kills this many people for ten thousand dollars. If it was millions, maybe, but not thousands."

She was right, Aaron thought. The deaths weren't motivated by money. It had to be the papers found in the suitcase. Or it could be the fact that someone stole from a rich guy, and he took it personally. There really was no way for anyone to know except for the guy doing the killing.

"Can you remember if Frank talked about the documents? Was there anything important in them?"

"He did mention that it was brilliant. I brought over his third beer of the night around eleven, and he told Joanne that the files were genius. 'Who would've thought? Those scientists.' Something like that." She narrowed her eyes, lost in thought. "Wait a second … there was something he said to your sister as I walked away. It was hard to hear as the music was so loud." Julie looked back at him. "Something about it had been going on for a long time. I heard the word 'years.' Then he said, 'the guy is getting crazy rich because of it.' I walked out of earshot by that point. I'm pretty sure that was it."

"You may have the answer. Whatever was in those documents may be enough to kill for. Do the police know any of this?"

She shook her head and fidgeted with her hands on her lap. "I gave them my statement about what happened at the club last night. That was all I could think about. I didn't think what Frank said to Joanne was all that important."

"I think it's what got him, and a lot of other people, killed."

Julie's parents kept a nice house. They looked like they had money. What happened to Julie that she would have to work in a strip club?

Julie had long, curly hair down past her shoulders, beautiful teeth, and a wicked smile. How he hadn't noticed how smoking hot she was before was a testament to how much stress he was under.

"Can you tell me what the cops think about last night?"

"I was waiting for you to ask. I thought that was the reason you followed the cop here."

"You saw me?" Aaron asked, surprised.

"Sure. I immediately knew your Nissan after yesterday morning when the bouncers headed out to scare you."

"And you didn't tell the cop? You weren't worried about me?"

She shook her head. "Not after what you and your friends did for us last night. I'd be dead if you hadn't come searching for answers, and that's what I told the cops. You're a hero. They're looking for you to get your version of events, but that's it, as far as I know. Even the bouncers are happy you put them all to sleep. Otherwise, they would've tried to play hero and get shot for it."

Relief swept over him. "You don't know how happy I am to hear that. I thought they'd be gunning for my head. I just wasn't getting any answers." Maybe it was time to meet up with Folley and tell him everything. "I guess I should be going. I probably need to get to the police station to give them my statement, too." He stood and slipped his hands in his pockets, suddenly shy in her presence.

"Yeah, I could use some sleep."

"Me too. I slept in my car last night. After everything went crazy, I didn't know what to do or where to go." He stepped around the coffee table and started for the front door. "Are you going to be safe here?"

She nodded, her eyes shutting briefly in her own subtle way. "Yes, as far as everyone's concerned, they've caught the bad guys."

"But what if the bad guy just sends someone else? I'm not trying to frighten you, but that's what I would do if I were the bad guy."

"Then teach me all that karate stuff," Julie said as she moved her arms up and down and in circles, trying to imitate Bruce Lee and looking like a human windmill. Aaron fought hard not to laugh.

"Were you going to laugh?" she asked. "Watch yourself. I could get you," she lunged in playfully, Aaron easily sidestepping her advance. He grabbed Julie, hugged her to him, and spun them in unison to the wall away from the front door. She gasped and settled into his arms for a moment.

Then the floodgates opened. It felt like someone had punched him in the stomach as he bent over and slipped to his knees.

"Joanne's dead," he mumbled, his lower lip shaking. "My sister is dead because someone stole a piece of luggage and went to where … she works and …" He sobbed, wiped his eyes, and tried to speak. Julie patted his shoulder in a gentle, consoling manner. "She was innocent," he continued, "I was going to get her out of that life. I'm sorry, I'm so, so sorry, Joanne. I should've done more."

Aaron lowered himself even further, lying on the

carpeted floor of Julie's house, and cried. He cried for all the missing years, for what his parents did to him and his sister, and for what society had allowed to happen to his family. It wasn't the best time to lose control—but he couldn't pick when his emotions would bowl over. Having not slept much, the adrenaline rush of last night gone, and discovering that his sister was probably killed to hide someone's secret, he lost control. How more unjust could the world be?

Julie walked away and came back a moment later with a Kleenex for him. He wiped at his puffed-up eyes, dabbing at the moisture collected around the lids. After a moment, he picked himself up off the floor, walked over, and eased back onto the couch.

"Why?" he asked. "Why did this have to happen? I loved my sister so much." The tears tried to break free again. It was the first time he had truly wept for Joanne since her voice message all those days ago.

"I'm sorry," Julie offered. "I can't imagine what you're going through."

He stared at the Kleenex in his hand, embarrassed that he had broken down in front of her. He needed to leave. He needed to be alone for a while, and then he needed to talk to Folley. After that, he would sleep at home, not in his car, and then he would find out who was behind the killing of his sister. Someone had to be accountable.

He rose from the couch and approached the hall. "I should go."

"You going to be okay?" Julie asked.

He nodded, still looking down at the Kleenex, twisting it through his fingers. "Yeah. I gotta deal with this." He met her eyes. "I can do it. It's just hard, you know. Real hard." The tears threatened again for a moment.

"I understand. Here, let me get you my phone number if you want to talk. You can call me. I'll get a pen and paper in the kitchen—"

Someone knocked on the front door.

Aaron slipped an arm around her waist, pulling her into him and away from the open hallway where anyone at the front door would see her if it were open. "You expecting anyone?" he whispered into her ear.

Julie shook her head. He could feel the fear coming off her as her body shook.

Could whoever was behind the carnage of the last few days work that fast? Did they have unlimited hitmen just sitting around waiting for the next assignment? Or was it a Jehovah's Witness spreading the word? If it was, he needed someone to punch.

She curled up inside his arms for the protection he offered. He could smell her, feel her, and yearned not to let her go.

No one is going to get this girl. Not with me around.

He moved his mouth down close to her ear. "Stay here. Don't move into the hall, or whoever is at the front door might see you through the shadows in the peephole."

She nodded and slipped out of his grasp. He eased up on the left side of the front window and knelt down. If the unknown visitor watched the living room window for movement, they would be staring at the height of where they would expect a head to be. They wouldn't be staring at the bottom left corner.

He moved the curtain back ever so slightly and, only using his right eye, peeked around the edge of the window's trim.

A man in a long black overcoat stood at the door, his hands clasped together in front of him. He wore black gloves on his hands, which seemed strange for this time of year.

The man knocked again. The human eye is drawn to movement, so Aaron turned slowly to look in the driveway and the road beyond but saw no vehicle. Maybe the man was a salesman of some kind doing his door-to-door thing. He could be a spreader of the Good Word, a religious freak, or even a nice neighbor asking for a cup of sugar. Whoever he was and whatever his intentions were, Aaron felt a certain unease.

Slowly, he angled his head to look at the unwanted visitor.

The man stared back at Aaron. He smiled and raised his hand. In it, there was a long piece of steel that glinted in the sunlight.

The gun fired.

Aaron barely had time to register what was happening. The sharp tone of glass breaking an inch from his face pierced the air. Wood chipped off the trim where his face had rested less than a second before.

He rolled onto his back, pushed into a roll, and flipped up, landing in his stance. Julie let out a short shriek before she covered her mouth and stared at Aaron as if he'd been shot. Her glazed eyes were wide in fear and shock.

"We have to go. Now," Aaron shoved her out of the paralysis of fear even while his legs turned rubbery. He hated the thought of dealing with guns. Why couldn't the goons show up with some other weapon?

He held Julie's wrist and guided her to the back of the

house. His mind raced over possible escape routes. He remembered the yellow house directly behind Julie's, but it was some kind of caged animal zoo. That wouldn't fare well.

When they reached the kitchen, he heard the bolt disengage on the front door.

"Shit, he's picking the lock."

Whoever had sent this man didn't want anyone alive knowing anything about what Frank Weeks found in that piece of luggage, Aaron was sure. These people were serious hired assassins who would stop at nothing. He was in way over his head.

"Is there an easy way out through the back? A fence we can jump or a path through to another backyard? Anything?"

Julie stammered for a moment, her eyes wild and unclear. She was losing self-control fast. He had to get her out of the house while she was still on her own two feet. Collapsing on him wouldn't be good.

Aaron glanced over his shoulder. The doorknob lock turned back and forth as the goon tried to gain access. They were down to seconds.

Aaron ran across the kitchen and ripped open the back door onto a patio. He motioned for Julie to come outside. She followed slower than he wanted, but he shut the door behind them once outside.

"Run to the back of your yard and climb the fence. Find shelter on that street and wait for me. Now go!"

"But what about you—"

"Go!" he ordered.

Aaron moved the barbecue out of the way so he could climb onto the deck's railing. He stood to his full height and grabbed the eavestrough on the roof's edge above his head.

With a strong push off with his feet, he lifted himself onto the roof's edge, kicked his right foot up so his leg was parallel with the ground, and then rolled onto the black shingles. He lay on his back, staring up at the clear blue sky. His heart raced as fear set in. It wasn't minutes ago that he was crying like a baby in Julie's living room, and now he was on her roof with a gunman inside the house, hunting them.

He couldn't move or risk any noise that would give away his position. He may already know, as Aaron wasn't sure how much noise he had made getting up or how close the gunman was.

He lifted his head and scanned the backyard.

Julie was nowhere in sight.

He hoped she got out of the yard. He needed her running down the other street, away from the danger.

Aaron knew this plan was dangerous, but he couldn't allow thugs to keep showing up with guns. Eventually, they would achieve their goal. He had to send the message that whoever they sent would end up in the hospital being questioned by the police.

He laid his head back, closed his eyes, and concentrated on breathing. He needed to calm down. He needed to be in control to have any chance of success.

A loud crash came from inside the house. His heart rate increased again, and he had to take deep breaths through his mouth. Beads of sweat rose on his forehead and face as the afternoon sun beat down on him. He rubbed his hands on his pants to keep them dry and waited.

The back door opened hard and slammed shut. Aaron had to assume the intruder was standing on the deck directly below him. He waited for a count of three and then slowly peered over the side.

The deck was empty.

Fuck.

He waited, listening. A minute passed. The only sound was the traffic in front of the house. No dogs barked, kids played, or adults argued in any of the houses nearby. It was like this one city block detected the danger and remained quiet, waiting for it to dispel.

Something moved below him. He chanced a look and caught sight of the man's arm. He stood near the barbecue.

He's good. If there was a trap, he waited for it to be sprung like a professional.

Aaron had moved the barbecue so he could jump to the roof. The man might be putting it together. He had to move away from the edge, jump onto the guy, or just see what he was doing now.

He needed to look first and then decide what to do. There was something about lying out on Julie's roof that suddenly didn't feel safe.

The man was gone when he edged around to look down at the deck. He leaned over farther and took in the whole deck.

Nothing.

If he climbed down, ran next door, and hopped the fence, he could call for Julie and make a run for his car. They could drive directly to Folley and have the police attend to the unwanted visitor.

Or was Aaron being played? Did the man figure Aaron was on the roof, and now he's sitting back, waiting for Aaron to climb down so he could shoot him? How smart and professional was the shooter?

Knowing he couldn't spend the afternoon on the roof, Aaron got in position to climb down. He removed his shirt and leaned over far enough to wave the shirt in front of the kitchen window. Getting a bullet in the shirt was a lot better than getting a bullet in the leg as he climbed down.

He waved it twice and got no response.

Does he think we ran away, so he's gone?

He put his shirt back on, took a deep breath, and lowered his legs over the edge. The black shingles smelled of tar. He hurriedly kicked below, searching for the railing to stand on. His right foot made contact. He applied pressure and put his full weight down on the railing.

Cold steel pressed against his right temple. Normally, Aaron would block a foreign object coming this close to his face this fast, but his hands were under his chest, supporting his upper body as he waited to step onto the railing. Now, though, any sudden movement would startle the gunman, who had climbed onto the roof and walked up behind Aaron.

"Where's the girl?"

"What girl?"

The intruder pulled a cell phone from his pocket, flipped it open, and aimed it at Aaron's face.

"Smile."

The cell phone clicked as the man took Aaron's picture.

"What's that for?" Aaron asked. "Your perverted picture collection?"

"I always take a photo of my victims a few seconds before I kill them to show proof of life. Then, I take a photo of the corpse. That way, I get paid without delay, and there's no confusion about how I did my job. Now, where's the girl?"

He dropped his cell phone back into his pocket.

"What girl? You want more pics for your masturbation session later?"

The intruder pulled the weapon back to pistol-whip Aaron with it. The second the gun lifted away from his temple, Aaron shot out an open-palmed right hand into the man's shin, right below the knee, searching for impact with the same nerves a doctor would tap with a hammer.

It worked. Before the gun could smack Aaron in the face, the intruder's leg jerked under him. He slipped to the roof's edge with a curse, about to fall. He let go of the gun, grabbed Aaron's shoulder, and held on.

Aaron turned to knock the hand loose, but the man's grip held. Both men lost their balance in unison, with the intruder going down first. Aaron tried to regain balance on the thin railing but fell to the grass five feet below. He landed hard, half on top of the gunman, who scrambled toward his fallen gun.

Aaron smacked the man in the throat hard enough to stop him but not hard enough to collapse his trachea. He sat on the gunman's stomach and twisted the man's arms under his knees, where they remained pinned.

Gasping with the fear, the fall, and the exertion, Aaron waited a few seconds before asking his first questions. The intruder tried to raise his legs high enough to pull Aaron off, but Aaron expected that move and elbowed both the man's knees, then drove two very hard fists into the intruder's stomach to remove the fight still inside him.

To encourage the intruder to answer his questions and stop squirming under him, Aaron grabbed the man's hair with his left hand, pulled hard enough to keep his head still, and then placed his right thumb over the man's eye and applied a soft pressure at first.

"Who are you?"

The eye not under Aaron's thumb bulged, but his mouth didn't move. He squirmed under Aaron, trying hard to get his head away from the prying thumb, but Aaron held firm and pushed harder. The free eye opened wide, and the intruder groaned.

"Who are you?" Aaron asked again.

The man tried to swing his head back and forth to dislodge Aaron's thumb, but Aaron's grip was too tight. Aaron had never actually popped anyone's eyeball out before, but he'd been trained how to. He wondered how that would look to the judge when he stood before him in court on the attempted murder charge. Then he wondered if he would even be in court if he didn't find out who these people were. Eventually, one of them would get lucky, and Aaron would join his sister. The thought of his sister made him push harder.

The man screamed and flailed under him. Aaron saw his thumbnail had dipped deep enough to be inside the man's orbital socket. Mucus mixed with clear liquid, and blood seeped out around his thumb.

"Tell me who you are and why you're here, or lose your sight completely. Might be hard to do your job blind."

The man squirmed violently and whimpered, more blood trickling past Aaron's thumb.

He lifted his thumb out and placed it over the man's other eye. As it touched down and started to press in, the man screamed.

"Okay, okay! Wait!"

Aaron eased off. A dog barked in the yard behind them. Aaron took a quick scan of the backyard but couldn't see Julie.

"The man who hired me ... is Clive Baron."

Aaron kept his thumb hovering over the man's one good eye. He looked like he was about to pass out. The bad eye wasn't as circular as it used to be. Aaron's stomach churned at what he'd done to the man's eye, but he could live with it.

"Who is Clive Baron, and why is he after Julie?"

"He's a billionaire ... imports vodka into Russia ... called and gave me a list of people to deal with ..."

Vodka? There's that connection again.

"Where's the list?"

"Memorized it ..."

Bullshit.

"How many more of you are there?"

"No ... idea."

The man was fading fast. The blood seeping from his open eye wound was slowing, but Aaron knew the pain in the man's head would be intense.

"Why does he want people killed?" Aaron asked. "Why not just leave us alone?"

The man's only good eye rolled up, and the lid closed, his head tilted slightly to the side.

Aaron lifted his knees off the man's arms and moved down his body, feeling for a wallet or ID. Aaron pulled a piece of paper from the man's pants pocket, a list of seven names and addresses in pencil.

Memorized it, my ass ...

Aaron shoved the list in his pocket and double-checked the rest of the man's pockets. Finding nothing else, he grabbed the gun off the grass and ran back through the house to the front door. After ensuring the front was clear, Aaron opened the door and walked along the sidewalk to the side street where he parked his car.

Julie stood from behind a bush ten meters to the right of his car and joined him at the passenger side door.

"What happened?" she asked. "Are you all right?"

Aaron nodded. "Yeah, close one, though. Come on, get in."

He opened the door for her and walked around to get in his side, hoping she wouldn't notice the gun he'd hidden in his waistband. Sitting in the car, he slipped it beside the seat controls by the door. If men continued to show up with guns, maybe he needed one, too.

"Where are we going?" Julie asked.

"To the police station."

"Why?"

"To report what just happened and to tell them about a man named Clive Baron."

"That's the name the cops were talking about at the station earlier," Julie said. "But I don't really know who he is."

"I don't know yet either, but I will find out. I swear, I'm going to find out."

Aaron pulled his cell phone out and called 911 to report the unconscious man in Julie's backyard.

Chapter 20

AARON PULLED INTO A parking spot at the police station. He hoped Folley would still be there. He didn't want to talk to anybody else.

They had talked on the way back to the station, mostly so Julie could calm down and understand what had just happened at her home. Aaron showed her the list, and Julie confirmed every name was either a waitress or a bouncer at the House of Lancaster except for the last two names. There was no address for the last two, just their names: Jackson and Hugh.

They both guessed that the two men Aaron and his friends stopped at the club were probably the two names on the list. Addresses weren't needed as both men were being held in jail, so the intruder, now referred to by Aaron and Julie as the assassin, knew where to find them.

"Let's go inside, tell Folley everything, and maybe he

can assign cops to watch the people on the list until this thing is over."

Julie nodded. The lines on her face were taut from the stress and fear in her eyes after finding out she was on the list. Aaron wanted to take all that fear and uncertainty away.

"You okay?" she asked.

He nodded. "Yeah. Let's go."

Folley walked out as they started up the front steps of the station.

"I've been waiting to talk to you," Folley said.

"I've been waiting to talk to you, too. Had something to clear up first."

"Yeah, what's that?"

"Had to stop another murder."

Folley stepped back, eyebrows raised. "What?"

"A man with a gun stopped by Julie's house because she's on the list."

"A gun? What man? What list?"

"Clive Baron has prepared an execution list, and the names on it include all the employees of the strip club where my sister worked. Also on that list are two names that might be the men who tried to blow the club up last night."

Folley squinted in disbelief. "Are you serious? How do you know about this list? How do you know about Clive? We just spent a lot of man-hours identifying him from sketches and Google Images. I think maybe you've got some explaining to do. How the hell do you know so much?"

"I have the list right here," Aaron said as he pulled it out.

"Where did you get it?" Folley asked.

"Off the man who came to kill Julie." Then Aaron leaned back and slapped his hands together. "Shit!"

"What?" Julie asked.

"I forgot to grab the guy's cell phone."

"Why is that so important?" she asked.

"He took a picture of me."

"He took your picture?" Folley asked, crossing his arms. "Why would he take your picture?"

"He said he always takes a picture before he kills his victim for proof of life, and then he takes a picture after he kills the person to prove to his employer that the job was completed. I should've grabbed the phone …"

"Julie, where were you when all this happened?"

"I jumped two fences to my neighbor's backyard and saw Aaron's car parked a block up. I hid in the bushes until I saw Aaron coming. I gave him two or three more minutes before I started knocking on doors to get someone to call the police."

Folley turned back to Aaron. "Where is this man right now?"

"He's in Julie's backyard, in need of medical attention. I called 911 on the way here to report it. Told them you were working the case and to call you with a heads-up."

Folley put his hands on his hips. "Will he still be alive when we get there?"

Aaron nodded. "Yeah, but he took a terrible fall off the roof. I think he's going to have eye trouble. When you send people to pick him up, ask them to grab that cell phone, will you?"

Aaron and Julie followed Folley inside the station. He talked to a dispatcher and told her to call his office when the units at Julie's house apprehend the intruder. Then, he motioned them to join him in his office.

Folley settled behind his desk. Julie took a chair by the

desk, and Aaron leaned against the wall by the door as he eyed the Rubik's Cube.

"Don't touch it," Folley said.

No one spoke for a moment, then Folley ran his hands through his thick hair and shook his head.

"This is serious shit," Folley said. "We have a lot of dead people, mercs downstairs in holding, billionaires hunting people for who knows why, and martial arts experts beating people up and saving lives. Can you tell me what's really going on?"

"What's a merc?" Aaron asked.

"Mercenary. A hired gun."

"Oh," Aaron said. He explained everything he had figured out so far. He started his research on the David Hornell Ferry all the way to following Julie in the police car and talking to her in her home about what happened at the club the previous evening. He explained why his three friends were there and how all he wanted was answers to Joanne's death.

"So what next?" Aaron asked.

"Pretty much everything you just told me I already knew. We'd gathered a lot through our interviews with the staff at your club," he gestured to Julie.

"It's not my club," she said.

"You know what I mean …"

"I won't be going back there. I'll find some other way to make money. I'm sick of getting my ass slapped by pigs, not to mention gunmen and bombs. I'm fucking done."

Folley cleared his throat and leaned back in his chair. His face changed. There was something Folley wasn't saying.

"What is it?" Aaron asked. "What's the next step? Are we

still in danger, or can you assign people to watch everyone on this list?"

"The best way to deal with this is to stop the person who authored the list. Remove the threat, and everything goes away."

"How do you do that?"

"Bump it upstairs."

"What does that mean?" Aaron asked.

"I handle missing persons cases. Because many of my case files were located at Casa Loma, I have paperwork filed for a temporary transfer to homicide where I could help Detective Wheeler and her team. But since this is above her head, this case will be out of our hands by the end of the day."

"What?" Aaron pushed off the wall. "Then who do we talk to? Why would they do that if you're the most familiar?"

"This is international. We're dealing with hired thugs from around the world, a rich British man living in Russia, and mass murder. Guys like me don't handle things like that."

"Great," Aaron said and threw his arms in the air. "I don't want to talk to random officers at different times. Who do I call if I run into trouble? I'm just getting used to you handling everything."

"You won't have to worry about that."

Aaron frowned. "Why not?"

"Your part is done. You're out of this. You've got enough trouble with your court case coming up in a few months. Just hope that John Ashcroft doesn't die in that coma or the charge gets raised to murder."

Julie spun in her chair to stare at Aaron.

"That's not fair," Aaron said. "Low blow."

Folley nodded. "True, but it doesn't excuse the fact that a man clings to life because of what you did to him. Then you're in the club last night with your friends, and now a guy *fell* in Julie's backyard. Eventually, something will catch up with you, and you won't be able to shirk it off."

Aaron looked at his shoes, mostly to avoid Julie's stare. She probably thought him a monster. How could he hurt someone so bad to put them into a coma and flip the bouncer in front of her, let alone escape an assassin with a gun, yet cry in her arms in her living room only an hour ago?

Maybe he was a monster. Maybe the pain of the past was creeping through, and martial arts was his excuse to let loose on a world that hurt him.

With water in his eyes, he looked up, avoided Julie's stare, and glared at Folley. "I don't give a shit about policies, cases, or what country the criminal lives in." He paused to wipe his mouth. "I lost my sister—my only family—and I'm going to find out who was responsible and make them pay, whether that means bringing them to you via a hospital or a coffin."

Folley stood. Cops didn't get intimidated as easily as the average guy.

"You will do no such thing. You will provide a formal statement," Folley smacked the top of his desk, "and then you'll go home, where you will remain until I can update you on the case. If you have a problem with that, I will contact your lawyer, Anthony Garrett, and discuss house arrest until your case comes to court. Don't test me, Aaron Stevens. You may be an amazing fighter, but you can't fight the law and win."

Aaron almost smiled as a song popped into his head. It was over. There was nothing left to say to Folley. He was giving up just like he did when Aaron first met him. Giving up before he even got started. He knew laziness when he saw it.

"You've got my statement. I just told it to you. And now I'm leaving." Aaron opened the door and stepped into the corridor.

He heard Folley coming around his desk and stopped to face him. Then the phone rang. Folley debated whether he should pick the phone up or fight with Aaron some more.

Decision made, he lunged for the phone.

"Yeah?" A pause. He looked at Aaron and then at Julie. "Yes, this is Folley." After a moment, "What? You've checked the whole place?" Folley hung up the phone. He sat down at his desk again.

Julie leaned over Folley's desk.

"What's going on?" she asked. "Who was that?"

Aaron came back into the room, leaving the door ajar.

Folley gave all his attention to Aaron. "The officers at Julie's house didn't find anybody in the backyard."

"What?" Aaron nearly shouted.

"They found what looks like bullet holes in the front door and a smashed vase in the kitchen, but no one was there."

"Impossible. He couldn't see out of one eye. The pain was too great. He passed out …" Aaron spewed his thoughts out before remembering what he'd told Folley when he arrived at the police station.

"I thought you said he fell from the roof."

"I didn't lie," Aaron said. "He did fall from the roof." He

showed Folley a small grass stain on his shirt. "I fell too. Landed on top of him."

"So what happened to his eye?"

"For a cop, you're asking the wrong questions."

"Oh yeah, what questions should I be asking?"

"You should want to know where this guy is. You should be on the phone, or whatever it is you guys communicate with, calling all cars in the area of Royal York Road to be on the lookout for a tall man wearing black gloves with blood and mucus dripping from a hole in his face where his left eye used to be. That's what you should be doing."

"Well, let me get right on that," Folley said, not moving. "Look, I'm a missing persons case file go-to guy. I don't hunt assassins in the streets of Toronto. That's someone else's job."

"Fine," Aaron said, his forefinger raised. "I'll do it."

He slipped out the door, closed it firmly, and ran for the front of the building. He cleared the stairs outside in one leap and made his car before Folley got outside.

Aaron squealed out of the parking lot, intent on gathering Daniel, Alex, and Benjamin again.

He needed them to finish the mess.

He needed them to help him find a way to get to Russia without a passport because Clive Baron was about to have an unwanted visitor.

Chapter 21

CLIVE BARON LOUNGED IN bed, waiting for Jessica to bring him his treat. It was nearly four in the morning, and he wanted to get up to see what was happening in Toronto as it would be around eight in the evening there. He wondered what the next boy would be like and fantasized about a young nubile. He hated body hair and hoped Jessica's choice would be hairless.

The phone rang beside him. He pushed down on his erection, applying pressure, and debated whether or not to answer the phone.

It rang again.

"What?"

The caller was out of breath. Clive heard panting, and what sounded like the caller was running.

"Hello?" he asked, sitting up in bed. "Who is this? How did you get through to this number?"

The phone in Clive's room only rang when Jessica put a call through. Whoever was calling had already spoken to his gatekeeper.

"Answer me, or I'm hanging up," he said. *And Jessica will lose a month's pay for this.*

"You bastard," the caller said through panting breath.

Clive could tell the caller wasn't running. It sounded like wind through an open car window, and the panting was grunts of pain.

"Identify yourself."

"You sent me after some kind ... of a fighter without telling me."

It was hard to hear the man speak as it sounded like he was talking through clenched teeth, but Clive picked up enough to determine it was Nick Sturnam.

"What the fuck are you talking about?" Clive asked as he stood and stared down at the phone's base.

"The list you emailed me ... the waitress had a boyfriend. And now I've lost an eye."

"It's all fun and games, now, isn't it? I'd suggest you continue with the list. You're still inside the twenty-four-hour mark."

"There will be no continuing with the *fucking* list."

"That is not a safe answer."

"Safe for who?" Nick asked.

"I'll be fine. I always win. I'm untouchable. You, on the other hand ..."

Clive waited for Nick to sign his own death warrant. He had access to many more professionals worldwide. Men he had employed in the past. Nick wouldn't make it to the weekend if he didn't appease Clive.

"If you're so untouchable, then why take out these people? How can they hurt you?"

"That's my business. Will you continue with the list, or do I assign a new team to my Toronto troubles?"

The sound of wind died down as Nick pulled his car over, Clive surmised. "I need something from you first."

"Go ahead."

"I'm a block away from a doctor that'll patch me up and shoot me up. When I'm done here, I need a name, address, and everything else you can get for me. This man has seen my face. He has to be cleaned up first. Otherwise, he may try to stop me again."

"Then you'll continue with the list?"

"With pleasure."

"The man you need identified … who is this person to you?"

"The man who protected the waitress and took out my left eye. I will email you a picture of his face. Find me a name. He goes first, then I finish your list. Deal?"

"I'll watch for your email, but I still want my demands met. Twenty-four hours, and the list is completed."

It wasn't a question. Clive knew Nick enough to know that he understood how serious the list was and the sense of urgency.

"Just get me a name," Nick said, and the connection clicked off.

Clive held the phone out and stared at it. When this was all over, Nick would have to go, too. He had proven to be a liability. He forgot who was in charge. There were thousands of men for Clive to hire in the future. That was the pleasure of his business; he had unlimited resources for exterminating.

The Americans, the Russians, and the Israelis were training his future mercenaries at that very moment. All Clive had to do was wait until their government left them on the battlefield, made them part of a cover-up story, or disrespected them in some harsh way. Then Clive would step in, offer a financial package and a lucrative deal any soldier would accept, and, poof, he had another hired gun. He'd done it over a hundred times in the last dozen years and would do it another hundred.

Nick Sturnam was as good as dead.

His computer beeped as an email came in. Wondering where Jessica was with his latest conquest, he ambled over to his MacBook and opened the email. The picture of a man in his twenties was attached, with green grass in the background. It looked like the photo was taken as the man was climbing off a roof.

He clicked the forward button and typed in his contact address at the FBI. Charles Beck worked with the Integrated Automated Fingerprint Identification System, IAFIS, the criminal history database maintained by the FBI. It was intended for law enforcement agencies and not the private sector, but Charles would get what Clive needed. If the man in the photo had ever committed a crime and was fingerprinted anywhere in North America, there was a high chance Charles would have the information back to Clive within an hour. If not, Charles would have the contacts to get a name for the man in the picture.

Then everything would come together. Nick would finish what he was hired to do, and Clive would have Nick removed in a way that left the authorities with someone to blame for all the recent murders in Toronto.

Clive hit send and opened a protected file that listed names of men he could bring in for various jobs. He eyed his Canadian contacts and found two men in Montreal. He figured they could be in Toronto by the following day. Perfect. Nick would just be finishing with the list.

He lifted his encrypted line to make the call, still naked, and wondered where Jessica was with his next nubile boy.

Chapter 22

Aaron drove for a few hours until he ended up in Hamilton. He drove up what the locals called Hamilton Mountain, found a mall on Upper James Street just after Fennell Avenue, and parked among the early evening shoppers' vehicles. He walked into the mall, hit a bank machine, and took out his daily limit. Then he pulled out his Visa and withdrew as much of an advance as possible.

Armed with just over two thousand dollars in cash, he walked to the food court in the small mall and found a Taco Bell. After loading up on two beef burritos and the five soft taco deal they offered that his daily workout regimen wouldn't allow, he returned to his car while he ate ravenously.

He had a decision to make and couldn't make it on an empty stomach. If he decided to go ahead with his plan, he needed cash and didn't want to take the money out of his account anywhere in Toronto.

He got on the highway and started back toward Toronto, headed to the hotel. He'd called Daniel and asked him to get Alex and Benjamin and check in at the Quality Suites Hotel near the Toronto International Airport. Aaron gave him specific instructions to have Alex check into the room. They were to wait for him there. When asked what was going on, he said something had come up—important enough that Alex should use his spy novel knowledge to ensure no one knew what room they were in. Daniel was confused, but Aaron told him not to worry about it. Alex would know what Aaron was talking about.

While driving through Oakville to Toronto, Aaron thought about his old high school teacher who quoted philosophical mentors. Mr. Gordon had memorized many famous quotes from Socrates, Plato, and Aristotle. Mr. Gordon had made them read The Republic, where they learned about the Philosopher Kings and Plato's school, The Academy.

The one thing that stood out all those years ago for Aaron was something Aristotle had said about evil. He said that evil was necessary. As necessary as the shadows of a beautiful painting, for without the shadows, the painting wouldn't have the same appearance or beauty.

Did that mean that men like Clive Baron were necessary? Was Clive a shadow? How were things more beautiful with men like that? With Joanne gone, Aaron felt rudderless. How could that ever be construed as beautiful? He'd lost his business, income, life, and now his sister.

What was left?

Each time he asked himself that question, the answer

kept coming back to Clive Baron. A rich man who thought he could do whatever pleased him that day. It didn't matter who he hurt or how he did it. The man was ultra-rich and powerful, but it had gone to his head. Whatever the Weeks brothers saw at the airport that started this domino death effect, it didn't matter as much as all the lives that were lost. Too many people were affected, too many lives.

Aaron thought of Joe Girard, the man who made the Guinness Books of World Records over ten years in a row for being the world's greatest salesman. He had many disciplines and other facts to back how he did it, but one thing that stuck with Aaron was Joe's *250 Rule*. Joe said, on average, approximately 250 people attended a funeral. That meant everyone has influenced or been involved with at least 250 people during their lifetime. For every murder Clive ordered, he was killing one human being and hurting over two hundred more.

Who could be allowed to wield that kind of power without consequence? Why was that allowed in a civilized society?

The only answer Aaron knew was that Clive Baron needed to be stopped, and he was the one who would stop him. He needed his friends to help him locate the country Clive was in and then decide how to get there since the judge took his passport as part of his bail terms.

He figured he had enough time to stop by his place for a change of clothes and still be at Daniel's by the time of the meeting.

He had kept the call to Daniel simple. He had asked him to research Clive Baron. When they got together later at the hotel, he had as much as he could on the man so they could discuss how to locate Joanne's murderer.

Daniel had more questions, but Aaron cut him short and said they'd talk that night at the hotel. Get the Russell brothers. They would work out a plan then.

Aaron entered the outskirts of Mississauga and headed for his apartment. He was on his way to a meeting with evil. He now knew what all the years of his martial arts training had been for. He understood his role, and he was prepared to play it.

There was nothing left to live for.

It was time to remove the shadows on the painting Aaron called life.

Chapter 23

Jessica had disappeared. Clive searched the outer office and walked through the rest of his condo but couldn't find her.

He walked back into his bedroom and sat at his desk. He tried her cell number, but no one picked up. He tapped his leg and drummed his fingers on the desktop.

Where could she be?

Why would she leave without telling him or leaving a note behind? He had been asleep, but she could've left him a note.

He tried her cell again, to no avail.

There would be consequences for this. He wouldn't tolerate insubordination. You teach people how to treat you by your actions. He would not ask where she had been or why she didn't leave him a note. Instead, he would cause her pain and then use her like he would one of his boys. After bleeding from the rectum for a few days, she'd remember to leave him a *fucking* note next time.

She had never done anything like this before. Since he had brought her on, she traveled with Clive, bunked with him, slept with him, and doted on his every whim. She even handled dead body disposal like a professional. Nothing shocked her.

She had a special phone number for a man who delivered boys to Clive. Little Russian orphans, lost or stolen orphans from a less fortunate country. Human trafficking has its benefits.

Clive often asked her if an orphan could eat in a family restaurant. Jessica never laughed.

She was off her post, late for her duties of supplying him with a new partner, and it was almost six in the morning. That meant she would be his partner instead.

Everything has its price.

He dressed and called his guards to meet him at his condo door. He was going out for an unannounced breakfast. With the Toronto issue being cleaned up, he needed to get back to business and show his employees there was nothing to worry about. If he stayed hidden and moved around too secretly, he could almost detect the worry oozing off some of his men.

The email notification on his computer dinged.

The computer took a moment to encrypt the message from Charles at the FBI. The image was of a man named Aaron Stevens. He had recently been charged with attempted murder in Toronto after putting a man in a coma. He was the surviving brother of Joanne Stevens, recently found dead at Casa Loma in Toronto.

"That's it." Clive snapped his fingers. "You wanker. I finally get to see the face of the man who has been pissing me off for days now."

Clive read the impressive file of Aaron Stevens and his short life. He fumed at the interference of one unarmed man against Mossad agents and hired assassins. It seemed impossible, improbable, but it was happening.

Nick was right. He had to take this guy out first.

But Clive didn't want that. He took a moment to formulate his response and decided that a lesson had to be taught. There could be no better way than to make it public for the world to see. His men needed a morale boost.

Clive was a lover of medieval things, such as leaving bodies in a turret of Casa Loma.

He was also a lover of the torture methods of those days. He would have Aaron brought to Palamidi in Nafplio, Greece, a popular tourist area. Clive would pay enough to have the site shut down for a few days, and then after an extensive question and answer session, with a torture and pleasure session added on, Clive would have Aaron drawn and quartered for the world to see.

Nothing was better than seeing the faces of the men who wanted to challenge Clive when they learned he was behind such brutality.

He tried Nick's cell phone but got no answer.

Then he clicked forward on Charles's email, blocked all information leading to Charles, and sent Nick an email with explicit instructions to not harm Aaron, except far enough to make him do as he was told. Clive would have a plane waiting at the Toronto Island Airport for Aaron to be delivered with Nick to Greece, where they would meet in

Nafplio. Pick Aaron up at his home address, which was supplied in the email, and make sure he gets on that plane. Clive explained that he needed to see Aaron's execution live. No pictures with this one. Nick would be paid five times his normal fee for the delivery of Aaron Stevens to the plane. After that, Nick was free to continue with the list.

His stomach growled, and he had lost his erection. Maybe it was better that Jessica hadn't been waiting with a new boy this morning. He was conducting much-needed business.

As he reached the door, his computer dinged again. For a moment, he debated whether to have breakfast first or see who emailed him.

Curiosity got the better of him. Another message from Charles.

He waited for his computer to open the encrypted email.

The first contained only one word.

Run.

The second line read;

Consider my debt to you paid. Once you read this email, even though it's encrypted, I will erase it from my system and destroy my hard drive with a hammer. We are done.

Jessica Nockler has ratted you out. A task force is set to move on you today in Moscow. I just found out. Something happened in Toronto that is linked to you. It raised their timetable. It's an early morning raid aimed at removing you from your Moscow condo at six in the morning today, Moscow time, which is twelve minutes from the moment I'm sending this email.

Be well.

Goodbye.

Clive looked at the clock.

05:49 a.m.

He erased the email and started the shutdown procedure of his computer. There wasn't time to be angry or frightened. He needed to leave the building as fast as he could.

He tossed a shirt over his head, slipped into his shoes, and jumped in front of his computer again. The screen was blank.

He secured his watch to his wrist.

05:52 a.m.

He pulled the PC's tower out from under his desk, laid it flat on the carpeted floor, and jumped on it. It took four tries to collapse the side of the tower far enough for him to see the hard drive had been torn from its moorings. As far as he could see, the damage was extensive.

05:54 a.m.

He grabbed his cell phone and called his men downstairs. Arnold, his main driver, answered, his voice measured.

He knows. The strike team is already in the building.

Heart racing, sweat beading on his forehead, Clive spoke into the phone, telling Arnold to meet him in the lobby. He wanted to take the car out to enjoy an early morning breakfast in Moscow.

Clive had backup plans for most unexpected events, but he'd never used them, nor did he know if any of them would work. The problem was that each backup plan had an escape route, a car, and a driver. He had never assumed all his men would be compromised. Without a driver, he had no way out. He didn't even have car keys.

There was no plan that involved getting out of his tenth-floor condo with an international strike force taking the building by storm, but he had to try something.

He grabbed cash he had stashed in the condo, his cell phone, and a gun and headed for the condo door. The camera by Jessica's desk showed no one was in the main elevator lobby outside.

He would have to open the door for part of his plan to work. If they were on the other side, he was done.

05:58 a.m.

He opened the door, held his breath, and entered the lobby. No one waited for him. He pushed the button of his private elevator, which always parked on the tenth floor. The doors opened. He stepped in, pressed the button for the lobby, and slipped back out. The elevator doors closed.

The elevator would take less than a minute to get to the lobby. When it got there, they would see it was empty and that he was on to them. That left him little to no time to execute his plan.

He pulled out his cell phone and texted the code entrusted to him years ago by the electrician who worked on the freight elevator. He walked away from his private lift and stood in front of the freight elevator. The code he typed into his cell would place the freight elevator into service mode. Then it would tell anyone watching the numbers that it was ascending to floor number twelve and not ten, where it would actually be going. The electrician made it so it would always show it was two floors above where it was.

With his eyes on the locked door to the stairwell, he waited, tapping his foot for the freight elevator to arrive.

06:01 a.m.

The freight elevator's door clicked and opened slowly. Clive entered and pushed the button for the basement parking level. The electrician who helped him orchestrate his escape plan all those years ago was long dead, never able to expose Clive's secret.

Maybe he'd kept Jessica on too long. Maybe she was disgruntled, feeling entitled. There wasn't an employee in the world who didn't feel entitled at some point. That led to a bad attitude, stealing, and insubordination among the staff. This is one of the reasons he changed his staff over regularly and used hitmen from a distance.

The doors closed, and he started to descend.

He knew if they did detain him today, he would be out tomorrow. His legal team would get him out and then build a case to put him back in the driver's seat. Jessica would end up dead of an apparent suicide, and so would Aaron Stevens and everyone else on the Toronto list, leaving no witnesses to testify against him.

This would all go away. Within weeks, he would be relaxing, a new secretary handling his affairs. He would also make a point of changing his staff more frequently. The stress of being hunted was not good for his heart.

The elevator slowed as it neared the basement. He smiled as he thought of the strike team watching the numbers and thinking the elevator was stopping on floor number two while he was one below the main floor. He leaned into the elevator's corner by the button panel with his gun gripped tight in his hand. As the doors opened, he flipped off the safety.

The darkness of the underground bled into the elevator.

Nothing happened.

No one tried to enter, and no demands were called out. He waited. In service mode, the doors would remain open until someone inside the car pushed a button. Slowly, to avoid making any noise or attracting unwanted attention, he wiped the sweat from his forehead and pushed off the wall.

A thought occurred to him. If agents were waiting for him in the gloom of the underground, walking out with a gun in his hand made him a target, and he didn't want to die with a bullet in the face.

He slipped his weapon into the back of his pants and slid around the corner of the elevator doors into the basement. This was the do-or-die moment. Either they would take him now, or they were too stupid to think he would go to the basement. He wouldn't put it past them to assume he had no idea they were in the building, that they were smarter than him. As far as he was concerned, the strike team was probably waiting for him to walk out in the lobby to meet his driver for breakfast.

The light from the freight elevator spilled out onto the cracked concrete of the basement parking floor. Small bulbs strung up by their wires lighted the area where cars were parked in dusty rows. He could hear water dripping somewhere to his right. Russian Ladas make up most vehicles in the dank lot one floor below street level.

Two men stepped out from behind concrete pillars, firearms raised above their heads, aimed at him.

"Down on the floor. Now!" one of them ordered in Russian.

He raised his hands shoulder height and played dumb, to his surprise. He responded with the strongest British accent he could muster at the moment. "I'm sorry, you have mistaken me for someone else. I don't speak Russian ..."

He moved sideways away from the line of fire of the man on the right.

"Down on the floor. Now!" the man repeated in perfect English.

"Oh ..." Clive feigned fear on his face and raised his hands higher.

The man to his right talked into a lapel mic in Russian. As far as Clive could tell from the distance of six meters, he was radioing someone to tell them they had the suspect in custody.

Oh no, you don't. Not yet.

"I'm just looking for my car ..." Clive said as he shifted to the left and dropped behind the boot of a Lada Sputnik.

A bullet pinged off the rear of the car, not one foot from his face. He pulled his gun out, leaned down on the dirty concrete floor, and shot the foot of the closest man. Reaching for his wound, the man wailed and fell to the concrete floor.

The man who had stood on Clive's right was now out of sight. Time was short. He had less than a minute before every strike team member in the building would rush into the basement.

He was out of options.

The freight elevator remained open.

He shoved his gun away, got to his knees, and shouted, "I'm coming out. Don't shoot. I give up."

The man with the foot wound had dragged himself behind a car, leaving a dark trail of blood behind. He could hear whimpering from that direction.

Clive raised both hands and stood to his full height beside the Lada.

Then he walked out into the open.

Chapter 24

AARON PULLED INTO THE parking lot of his apartment building, searching for anything unusual. The sun was setting, the evening lights casting an orange glow over the lot filled with the tenants' vehicles. He drove the length of the lot twice, passed his own spot, and then parked in visitors.

He turned the Nissan off and waited, listening to the ticking of the hot engine as it cooled from the two-hour drive to Hamilton and back.

A four-door sedan, the model hard to make out in the dusk, pulled in, drove past him, and parked a dozen cars away. The driver got out, laughed, and slammed his door. A woman stood from the passenger side and joined him at the trunk, where they embraced and shared a long kiss. Hand-in-hand, they walked to the side door of the building, used a key, and entered.

Nothing else moved. He understood that the police could

be waiting for him, but what scared him more than the police was whoever hunkered in the shadows with murderous intent. Clive sent the two men to the strip club with instructions to murder everyone. The intruder showed up at Julie's home shortly after that. That meant two things. Clive knew where everyone lived and wouldn't stop sending hitmen until the job was done. Of all the people Clive wanted to remove, Aaron topped the list.

No amount of training could teach Aaron how to block a bullet. Guns meant no real defense. That's what scared Aaron.

Maybe coming to his apartment was a bad idea. He could get clothes elsewhere. He didn't have a passport or any other real need to go to his apartment. It was only out of habit.

"Fuck it."

He started the car and backed out of the parking spot.

A large GMC SUV slowed and pulled into the parking lot. Aaron had never memorized all the cars at his building, but he was sure he had never seen an extended SUV before. It drove toward him slowly and passed by.

He accelerated, hit the road, and drove away.

Three blocks later, the headlights of an SUV appeared behind him.

"No way ..."

How could they work that fast? If they did, and it was the guy with the missing eye or some other hitman, there was no way to outsmart them. Clive just had too much money. Folley couldn't fly over to Russia and arrest the man.

Aaron drove faster, then slower. He took two unnecessary rights and then three lefts. The SUV stayed with him at least two car lengths back.

Unless he wanted to hit the highway and try to outrun the SUV, he wouldn't lose the tail. His stomach rebelled. Years ago, he had lost his fear of confrontation at sparring matches and tournaments. He was perpetually ready for and willing to fight if needed, but hired hitmen with guns were real life and death, and that scared him.

The only way to lose the tail would be to meet with Daniel and the Russell brothers and take them to another meeting spot.

He turned onto the 427, heading south toward Toronto's International Airport and the Quality Suites. He hoped Alex had checked in as he had directed.

The SUV stayed with him, accelerating without trouble on the busy highway.

A part of him wanted to slam on the brakes and have the SUV ram his back bumper, lose control, and crash in a ball of flame on the side of the highway. Maybe the way to deal with these kinds of people was how they dealt with things: with extreme prejudice and over-the-top violence.

But that would put innocent lives at risk, and he wouldn't do that, which was the problem with the scale. It weighed heavily in their favor. They didn't care who got hurt to take down their target, while the good guy had to stay alive with minimal damage to himself and his surroundings.

Aaron watched his mirrors and kept his speed under control. He took the exit ramp to the airport. It turned into Dixon Road near the hotel, but he forgot exactly where.

The SUV followed without pause. The driver couldn't be more obvious. Aaron did not doubt what was happening. His would-be executioner was driving the vehicle behind him, waiting for his prey to place himself unknowingly into his sight, where he would pull the trigger and send Aaron to see his sister.

The only way to get out of the target range of the unlimited supply of hitmen was to kill Clive. He couldn't believe he would think that way, but the circumstances called for it. Within one or two more attacks, it would be Aaron who would lose. He would get stung by bee after bee until he succumbed unless he could find a way to get to the queen bee and destroy the hive. A seemingly impossible task, but he had to try.

He turned left onto Carlingview Drive and immediately turned left again, pulling into front of the Quality Suites. He backed into a spot a few down from the main doors and jogged into the lobby before the SUV turned in. Over his shoulder, the large vehicle lumbered into the parking lot raced across and screeched to a stop beside his car.

"Can I help you?" the man behind the counter asked with a genuine smile.

"Alex Russell would've left a message for me. My name is Aaron Stevens."

The SUV's doors were just shutting.

"Ahh, yes, he said to give you this."

The clerk handed him a folded piece of paper. Aaron opened it to read room number 432. He handed it back to the clerk.

"Men are coming in behind me. Give them this paper." Aaron backed away and jogged down the short hall for the elevators. An older couple was waiting for the elevator, and the light red lit up around the button. The elevator descended to the second floor on its way to the first.

Aaron moved behind the couple to block the view from

the front lobby door. The doors slid open, and the intruder from Julie's house stepped into view, a large white bandage taped across his left eye.

Holy shit!

Three burly men followed him in.

The elevator doors opened. People filed out. Aaron followed the couple on. Before entering, head down, he looked at the intruder, who scanned the lobby as he approached the front desk.

The elevator doors closed. The couple had pressed the seventh floor. Aaron pressed the number two. Room 432 actually meant room 234. The spy novel reference Alex would've known was to switch the number. Alex read it over a year ago in a novel and talked about it for months with Aaron, covering all the details of being in an action-adventure. Alex lived this fantasy life through video games and novels. Aaron knew that if they were checking into a hotel, there was almost no doubt Alex would leave a note with the room numbers reversed.

Aaron jumped off when the elevator stopped on the second floor. He hustled down the hall to room 234 and rapped on the door hard.

"Who's there?" Daniel's voice.

"It's me, Aaron. Open up."

"Come on in," Daniel said as he opened the door. "The gang's all here."

"We have to leave. Now. I was followed here. Four guys are in the lobby and aren't here to have tea with us. We have maybe one minute. No doubt they're on their way to the fourth floor, thanks to Alex. Guys, gather your things. We'll take the stairs and use my car. Let's go."

"What's going on?" Daniel asked as Alex and Benjamin walked up behind him.

"No time to explain. We have to move." Aaron rushed down the hall but paused when none of the three followed him. "What's up, guys? We gotta go."

"Maybe this is too big a fight, Aaron," Benjamin said. "Can't the police handle it—" He broke off when Aaron stepped inside their comfort zone.

Aaron's face tightened. "My sister was murdered. The man responsible has four men in this hotel looking to kill me. I had a gun"—he pointed a finger at his temple—"placed here hours ago. I'm lucky to be alive. After talking to the *police*, there isn't much they can do. The bad guy lives in Russia. Basically, I'm a walking dead man. I will not go down without a fight, as it is my life we're talking about now and not just Joanne's. I want you three on my side. If this is too much, stay here for the night and then go home. I'll understand. But if you're with me, follow me now because I need you guys."

Aaron leaned on the door's trim. Precious time ticked by. His pursuers would be on the fourth floor by now and realize they'd been duped. They would either return to Aaron's car or wait for him in the lobby. Perhaps they saw the elevator stop on the second floor, not the fourth. Or maybe they were already by his car, waiting.

Shit! I should have pushed the fourth-floor button.

Aaron dipped his head out the door and looked down the hall in both directions. Still empty.

When he looked back at his students and friends, they weren't coming. He should have expected it. This was bigger than training in the martial arts. This was international murder, assassins, and real-life violence. People had been killed and could be killed. How could he expect anyone to join him on his personal crusade? It was a dream of his that the best fighters of his dojo would join him in the biggest fight for justice of his life, but he could see by the expressions on their faces and the tension that suddenly filled the air they weren't coming.

"It's okay, guys. Forget it."

Aaron moved into the corridor, followed by Alex. He wasn't coming along, just wanted to wish him well.

Aaron ran to the end of the hall and opened the stairwell door. Alex waved to wish him well. Aaron waved back.

"Thanks," he said loud enough for Alex to hear and then disappeared behind the door.

He felt let down and saddened by this turn of events. He actually thought the four of them could chase Clive Baron to the ends of the earth and beyond as a team.

His friends hadn't let him down, but he felt let down just the same. They had every right to deny his request to join his fight. Alex worked at Taco Bell and was saving his money to open his own franchise. Daniel and Benjamin worked on forklifts at a factory in Etobicoke. They were great fighters, the best, but they were Toronto boys, waiting for the weekend and the next beer with buddies, not a fight with the next international criminal gang.

Aaron hit the first-floor landing and almost laughed. He was running for his life and needed to pay someone back for the hotel room, whether in trade with private lessons or cash, depending on who paid for the room. Alex would take payment in lessons, but the forklift drivers were always short on cash.

He slowly opened the door to the lobby. Nothing threatening or suspicious. He slipped out of the stairwell, across the open lobby, and made it to the main doors before he stopped.

No sign of his pursuers. He assumed they were still on the fourth floor or on their way back down to the lobby. They wouldn't know where his friends were, and after he left, they wouldn't be able to follow him as *he* didn't even know where he was headed.

Maybe back to the police station, or maybe he'd contact Julie. He felt directionless. There was nothing he could do, and he had no idea where to go to do it.

Clive Baron had to be his next task. Find him, get to him, and end this nightmare. But how?

The night air had cooled. Several cars down, a man fumbled with his keys by a four-door Cadillac while holding a piece of luggage over his shoulder. A woman held a cup of coffee on a bench by the walkway and puffed on a cigarette. No one else was in the immediate area. He crossed toward his Nissan and pushed the button to unlock the doors. The familiar beep sounded.

As he opened the car door, he caught a shadow behind him. He raised an arm to block the sudden movement to his right. He screamed in pain as a steel pipe broke his wrist on impact.

The pipe came down again.

Aaron collapsed to the concrete, silenced.

Chapter 25

CLIVE STOOD IN THE space between the Lada and the open elevator doors. The other strike team gunman, covered in body armor and helmet, poised behind a concrete pillar.

"I'm done. You've got me," Clive said as he sidestepped as if dazed.

"Stay where you are." The gunman moved from behind the pillar, only far enough to keep his weapon trained on Clive.

Clive pretended to have weak legs, stumbling to his right to move closer to the open elevator door, but the gunman caught the movement.

"Drop to the floor. Do it now! Hands over your head."

Clive stepped sideways once more, knowing he was pushing the guy to shoot him. If he got shot, it was all over.

"I've got a detonator," Clive shouted. "Don't shoot. The whole building could blow. Let me throw it to you first. I don't want to die," he said in his most convincing voice.

"Last chance. On the ground, now!"

"I can't," he shouted back. "The detonator is in my pocket. I'll just get it out first." Clive lowered his hand and touched the top of his jeans pocket. He nodded toward the shooter. "It's okay. Just getting it out. Once I toss it toward you, I can get on the ground. If this button is pushed, we'll all die."

He wondered if the strike team member was buying his story. He probably didn't, but he hadn't shot yet, which was what Clive was bargaining for. The man also knew that dozens of his friends were heading to the parking level to back him up.

"Shoot him," the wounded man called from the left.

"I wouldn't do that if I were you. The button can be pushed quite easily."

Clive reached inside his pocket and grabbed his room key. He slowly lifted it to the edge of his pocket. The open door to the elevator was still six feet away.

"Once I toss it to you, I will get on the ground."

A door opened somewhere to his right. Another door. The shuffling footsteps of dozens of men filed into the basement parking area.

He pulled the room key out completely. Behind the shooter, men rolled into the basement parking area in waves and dropped behind cars.

He tossed the key toward the shooter, took two large steps to his right, and dove for the open elevator, punching the button for the third floor. A weapon discharged. Then another. A bullet ricocheted above his head. He had no idea how many men were coming toward the open doors.

More bullets pinged off metal.

The doors began to shut. Each second they took, he expected a weapon or an arm to jam between them. But nothing came, and the doors closed, muffling the continued pinging sound.

The elevator lifted. When he reached the third floor, the elevator's display would say he was on the fifth, but he wondered if the men chasing him were quick enough to have figured it out this time.

He pulled out his cell phone and texted the code to turn the freight elevator off service, which would correct the readout in the building. When he exited on the third floor, it would accurately say the third, and the strike team would assume he was in the lobby.

The doors opened on the third floor. No one waited for him.

The power went out. The elevator's interior lights blinked off. The entire area went black. A second later, emergency exit lights flickered on.

He pulled out his weapon and ran down the hall to the apartments that overlooked the small market store on the street. At apartment 302, he knocked hard.

"Superintendent," he yelled in Russian. "Open up."

He waited, watching the hall behind him. The door opened an inch, and an old woman stared at him through the chained opening.

"You're not the superintendent—"

Clive body checked the door, broke the chain, and knocked the old woman into the wall. She sprawled onto the tiled floor, where she gasped for breath.

He didn't have time to gag or bind the old woman.

He threw back the curtains, kicked a wire plant rack out of the way, and slid the balcony doors open. The railing was a wall of solid metal about three feet high. He crouched so no one could see him from below, crab-crawled to the edge, and peeked over.

Police cars filled the street half a block up near the entrance to the building. Directly below, pedestrians walked by or entered the market.

He tucked his gun in the small of his back and climbed over the edge. The drop was too far for his age and physical condition. The longer he hovered outside the balcony railing, the more attention he would receive. But surrendering now, after shooting one of theirs, he would probably spend more than a day in a holding cell, possibly longer.

He had to drop down and run to fight from afar. This was his only chance. His last chance.

He edged left, then right, trying to set himself just a little off-center of the large red awning over the market. The peaches and plums would be in their normal spots in the center.

Clive let go and braced himself. He fell, angling sideways so his right shoulder would take the impact.

The awning bent in the middle as he hit, slowing his descent. Metal popped. A metal arm bent and then cracked. He free-fell again, but only for a fraction of a second before he hit the peach stand dead center. Hundreds of peaches crushed under his weight, breaking his fall enough to avoid any broken bones, but his right calf smacked the edge of the peach container.

Clive yelped and then clamped his mouth shut. He rolled off the display case and tried to stand. He collapsed to his knees, not so much from the pain in his leg but from the fear of having performed such an act at his age. He felt weak, even though adrenaline flowed freely through his veins. He tried to get to his feet again, wondering if he could.

People around him gasped, and someone yelled inside the market. The electricity was out in the store. They had tried to slow his movement without electricity, but they were too late.

The commotion would attract attention. He needed to move, and he needed to do it fast. The owner came out of the market, bellowing in Russian. Clive leaned against a shelf and pulled out a small wad of bills, tossing them at the small man who slowed his barrage to look at more money than he probably saw in a year.

With all the strength he could muster, he moved. His legs worked better with movement. None of the strike team followed him yet.

One block down, his heart slowing enough that he didn't feel he would die of a burst valve, he pulled his weapon out of his belt line and stepped onto a side street.

A small convertible BMW, not usually seen in these parts, pulled up to the corner. He aimed the pistol at the driver's head and ordered her out.

A middle-aged woman opened the door tentatively and climbed out, heels clacking on the concrete. She was about to say something when Clive smacked her across the mouth. She staggered back and leaned against a car parked on the side of the road. He jumped into her BMW and slammed the door behind him. He tossed his gun on the passenger seat and dropped the clutch, turning right, away from his building.

In the rearview mirror, armed men in full Kevlar vests

and helmets ran to the fresh fruit market to investigate the downed awning.

He smiled at himself in the mirror and headed for the airport to meet Aaron.

He had a special prison in Nafplio, Greece, that Aaron would call home during the last few days of his short life.

Chapter 26

AARON LIFTED OUT OF a pain-filled dream. The ground moved below him. He adjusted his body to counter the movement, but pain paralyzed him into immobility.

He clenched his teeth and moaned, squeezing his eyelids closed. He hadn't opened them yet, afraid of what the light on the other side of his lids would do to his roaring headache.

Thoughts of the Quality Suites, the pursuit, and the man hidden behind his car ran through his mind. The pipe.

He opened his eyes to slits. He was lying on his back in a vehicle, trees racing by the windows. It was either a van or a makeshift ambulance. Wires or IV lines hung from hooks, and a stethoscope rested from the knob of a small cabinet that held numerous small bottles with labels on them.

He tried to lift his good arm, but something held him down. He tried again, his strength all but spent.

What have they done to me?

He tried to lift his head, but it was too heavy.

"Hey, the asshole's awake."

A man came into view. His lips curled up, and his face skewed in an angry scowl.

Do I know you? Aaron tried to ask, but his mouth didn't move.

Music played from the vehicle's radio. A truck raced by going the other way, the wind swooshing the small van.

The man touched the wires dangling above Aaron's head. Aaron tried to see what the man was doing.

"Fuck off!" the man shouted at Aaron.

He leaned closer, smiled, and lifted his hand in the air for Aaron to see it. Everything in Aaron's body fought to move, counter the strike, and manage the man in front of him bodily, but nothing worked.

The man's hand dropped hard and fast. His fist crossed Aaron's cheek and grazed his teeth as it passed. Aaron's face whipped sideways, the pain immediate and intense.

Aaron groaned, but nothing else in his body responded to his brain's commands. He had never felt so paralyzed, so out of control.

The man laughed, a long and hearty guffaw. He smiled in Aaron's face, showing off the yellowed teeth of a smoker.

The man touched Aaron's face with his finger and withdrew it to show Aaron what he had done. Blood covered the edge of the man's fingernail.

"Not bad, eh? Just wait; in the next little while, you'll learn what real pain is. Do you think popping a man's eyeball out is bad? That's nothing to what you're going to go through."

The man drew back his arm, then dropped it hard and

fast again. This time, Aaron lost consciousness.

***

Nothing moved under him when he came to. With care, he opened his eyes and looked around. He touched his tongue to his swollen lip. One tooth felt out of place. The only plus was the pain in his head had subsided some.

They had propped him upright in a wooden chair, his hands tied behind his back, ankles bound to the legs of the chair. From the neck up, his head was free. He turned slowly and examined the chair. The wooden edges were trimmed with metal, and the chair was reinforced to maintain durability.

Moonlight shone through a window to his left, lighting the dirt floor enough for him to see he was in an unfinished building or a condemned structure.

There was nothing else to see in the dark. He couldn't detect anyone close or any movements.

Hunger gripped his stomach, and his bladder screamed for release. He wore only his underwear, but fortunately, the temperature in the building was quite warm. His underwear was already soiled.

Whoever brought him here hadn't cleaned him. All they had done was strip him, tie him up, and leave him in his own filth.

Who does this kind of shit? What the fuck is this?

"Hello," he called out in a cracked voice.

He struggled against his binds to no avail. It would do no good if he could knock himself down or try to bang the chair against the floor or the wall. The chair was too strong. They had to be certain the chair would hold to leave him here tied up, unattended. And he had to be far from others, or they would hear him scream when he woke.

Think, dammit, think.

The pain returned slowly. First his broken wrist and then his head.

They drugged me ...

As the narcotics wore off and the minutes clicked by, the pain came on, stronger than any pain he'd ever felt before. He groaned, closed his eyes tight, and willed the pain away. He tried to move the fingers of his right hand, but it hurt too much. He moved the fingers of his left to examine his broken wrist. Something hard and covered in thick sticky liquid stuck out of the skin by his wrist.

His empty stomach revolted, and he hurled a chunk of bile out. He spat a dark, bloody lump onto the moonlight-carpeted floor.

He was in a den of lions. These men had the advantage, and they knew it. There were many of them and only one of him. Wherever he was, only the men who brought him here knew of his whereabouts. He was wounded. Possibly fatally, depending on what they'd been pumping into him. The fight he had put up in Toronto had been for his life, so it had been vicious and necessary. Now that they had the advantage, they would exact the same kind of violence on him with extreme prejudice.

He shook with fear—the fear of pain and death—a natural fear that humans felt at the end.

He controlled his breathing, lowered his chin to his chest, and closed his eyes.

Then he released his bladder. The warm liquid moved out

around his buttocks and dripped off the chair, running down his calf muscles.

He wondered how appropriate it was that he just pissed himself.

I'm a cliché. He willed sleep to take him from this hell.

Chapter 27

THE AWE-INSPIRING FORTRESS of Palamidi perched in regal beauty atop the large, rocky hill over two hundred meters above Nafplio, Greece. Built in the late 1600s and completed before 1715, the fortress was a huge task, incorporating all the experience the Greeks had available to them at that time. Bastions had water reservoirs, munitions depots, food storage areas, frequent moats, machicolations or *murder holes*, outer retaining walls, and barracks. For its day, it was a marvelous piece of work. Today, it's a tourist attraction with thousands of visitors yearly.

Clive Baron looked up at the expanse of steps that led to the top of the fortress. Local legend held that there were 999 steps, and one was broken by a soldier's horse and never repaired. Items on restaurant menus use this number to attract tourists' eyes.

But Clive loved history and had visited Palamidi before.

He knew there were actually 857 steps from the street level to the edge of Palamidi and more than a thousand to the top.

"Go," Clive ordered his driver. The sleek Mercedes moved away from the center of Nafplio and drove past the fresh fruit and fish market that popped up every Wednesday and Saturday en route to the access road to the top of the hill where Palamidi sat. Tour buses moved slowly past the market, and Greek farmers walked back and forth across the road, selling and shouting out the prices of their produce. Clive smiled. None of these people would ever experience his wealth.

The day the strike team attacked his condo, he had made it to the private Vnukovo Airport in Moscow and chartered a plane that took off within an hour. They'd landed in Rome to refuel, altered their flight plan, and continued to the Athens airport. On the way, he had negotiated the use of the Fortress of Palamidi for two days for a private party. With the economic crisis, the Greek government was happy to accommodate him and his considerable contribution to their political party.

Using a secured line on the private plane, he had his men take Aaron Stevens to Palamidi and place him in the second bastion, just to the right of the main entrance.

They arrived late last night and stopped drugging Aaron, per Clive's instructions. He wanted him awake for this morning's first interrogation in honor of a prisoner's interrogation hundreds of years ago.

Clive wondered if Aaron really had any idea what he had in store for him.

The driver started up another street that led to Karathona Beach. Near the top of the hill, he turned to the right, up the winding slope to Palamidi. Clive wondered how many vehicles had slipped over the edge with no guardrail, the town a two-hundred-meter drop below.

At the top, the driver pulled up to the gate guarded by Clive's men. Weapons were well hidden in case any members of the public didn't know that it was closed for a private affair and wandered up. All vehicles were redirected as soon as they approached.

The driver opened Clive's door. Clive's forehead beaded with sweat when the oppressive heat hit him.

"Provisions stocked up?" he asked.

The guard who approached the vehicle nodded.

"Take me to the prisoner," he said in the most official tone he knew.

This was his playtime, his *let my hair down* time. When bored, he would tour ancient ruins and castles and marvel at the tales of torture and how the people of days long forgotten had lived.

He followed the guard through the main gates, the same one all the tourists entered, and then to the right, toward the second bastion.

Palamidi was built in the typical Baroque style. It was freed from the Turks on November 29, 1822. The Greeks entered through the Achilles Bastion, which, by its name, depicts the weakest bastion for defense. At one point on the stone wall on that side, it is not much higher than three meters.

Clive stopped at the door, where he admired the architecture. The sun shone down from a cloudless sky, beating his back in a soundless cry for him to enter the dark recess of the cooler prison cell. Clive relented, entered, and waited for his eyes to adjust.

In the center of the room, Aaron Stevens sat on a wooden chair, ankles bound to the chair's legs, arms twisted behind his back, and a single rope wrapped around his chest.

He didn't lift his head or acknowledge Clive's presence.

I'll break you soon enough, Clive thought.

He motioned for his men to leave. The guard who had escorted him here waited by the door as Clive instructed the men never to leave anyone alone with Aaron.

"You have proven to be a problem for me."

Aaron didn't move.

"Are you asleep?"

Aaron lifted his head and glared at Clive. "You are a dead man. Talking to you is a waste of time."

Clive almost stepped back. No one ever said anything remotely close to words like that to him. The nature in which the words were spoken reminded Clive of the Spartans. Maybe Aaron had Viking or ancient Greek blood, as he had shown himself to be quite the warrior.

"You have made mistakes," Clive said as he walked around to the back of Aaron's chair. Blood surrounded Aaron's wrists. He smiled at the broken right wrist. "And you just made another one. It is not me who is the dead man. It is you." He made it full circle and stared down at Aaron. "Many great men were held in this prison. Did you know this was the cell of lifers hundreds of years ago?"

Aaron lowered his head.

"That's right. Theodoros Kolokotronis was a hero in the Greek Revolution in 1822. He was held prisoner in the same room you're in now. The Miltiades Bastion served as a prison for those serving life sentences. Theodoros was executed for his crimes as a result of a civil war that broke out during the Independence of Greece. Did you know any of this?" Clive grabbed Aaron's hair and yanked his head back. "You're going to listen to me, or you'll wish you were dead. The pain I will cause you …"

Aaron spat, the phlegm hitting Clive's cheek. Clive wanted to shoot Aaron in the face for that, but he controlled himself. He wanted to have fun and enjoy the process. He couldn't allow the prisoner to win and have an easy death.

"I want to see my sister," Aaron said.

Clive pulled out a handkerchief and wiped the saliva from his face. "Your sister is dead."

"Are you fucking stupid?" Aaron shouted.

Clive stopped wiping his face. "What did you just say?"

"I asked if you were stupid. I know my sister is dead. Kill me so that I can see her again."

Clive took a deep breath. He tossed his handkerchief aside and moved behind Aaron. The blood had congealed around the split skin of the wrist, a piece of bone protruding with a jagged edge.

Clive leaned in with his finger and thumb, gripped the small bone, and held tight.

"This is what you get for your disrespect."

He twisted hard, yanked down, and pulled as if using a joystick to play a video game. The effect was more split skin and a renewed gush of blood.

Aaron's wail chilled Clive but also rekindled his spirit. He didn't get to do this that often anymore. There were always too many people around. The boys Jessica had brought him routinely were almost always smothered, a quiet closure to the pleasure they offered him in their short time together.

The real joy was in torture, and at Palamidi, he could have Aaron yell as loud and as hard as he wanted for days. Even if a police officer drove up the access road to investigate a noise complaint, Clive's men would apologize and excuse it as rowdy partygoers.

The Greeks are the noisiest culture I know. They won't care or notice.

His whereabouts were covered, too. When the private plane landed in Rome, he officially exited the plane. Anyone searching for him would assume he was lost in Rome somewhere and search among the ruins of the Coliseum and the Spanish Steps. No one would think he was in Nafplio, once the capital of Greece, before Athens took that title.

He released Aaron's wrist bone. Aaron had passed out.

"Pity. I was just getting started."

Clive left the room and stepped out into the sun.

"I'm going for a nap. Is my room made up?"

The guard at the door nodded. "Yes, sir."

"Good. I'll be back when the sun sets. It's just too hot for torture, don't you think?"

"Yes, sir."

"Make sure he is awake when I return and have smelling salts available. I will need a hammer, too. It's going to be a long night."

Clive almost started singing to himself. He had been lucky to get away from his pursuers in Moscow. Now, he was in Greece, and no one would find him. He had access to millions of dollars in accounts that couldn't be traced to him, and a private jet sat on a runway not far from Nafplio, awaiting his return.

The world wasn't just his oyster. It was his play toy.

***

Clive entered Aaron's prison cell as the sun dipped below the Greek mountains behind him. In preparation for the evening's festivities, after waking from his nap, he had dined on dolmades, vine leaves stuffed with rice, saganaki, a breaded and fried cheese, and moussaka, a traditional Greek dish. He even sampled red wine from the nearby Nemea region.

Aaron had been given nothing to eat. Clive wanted him in a weakened state. It was Aaron's strength in Toronto that brought him here, and it was Aaron's strength that would cause his death. Clive had devised a way to cripple Aaron's martial arts abilities and was excited to start the evening off with a wonderful show for his men.

The only thing that still concerned Clive was that he hadn't gotten ahold of Nick Sturnam after he had followed Aaron to the Quality Suites Hotel in Toronto. His men had delivered Aaron to the waiting plane at the Island Airport as ordered, but Nick had failed to report in.

Clive had called his Russian legal team on the plane from Rome and informed them about the raid. He wanted to know what they were looking for and what possible charges they had.

Then, he contacted a man he had known in the RCMP in Canada for over fifteen years. He asked him to check into the Toronto situation and report back to him on Jackson, Hugh, and Nick Sturnam. The last he had heard was Nick had gone to the Quality Suites Hotel by the Toronto International

Airport. He asked his contact to find out what he could and call him back on his encrypted cell phone. That particular contact had proven difficult, and he protested, but Clive reminded him that he still had men in Toronto who could cause a most unusual accident.

The last he heard was that Jackson and Hugh were still in custody, and the staff from the strip club were all still alive and kicking.

Maybe I'll have to go back to Toronto and handle everything myself.

A large fan was connected to a long black extension cord that roped through one of the windows, over the outside wall and plugged into the main building that handled the ticket sales for the fortress. Temporary lights had been brought in.

Aaron, paler than before, sat in the same position. His skin had taken on a white tone as his body weakened from a lack of food and the intense pain he had endured.

The dirt beneath the wooden chair had darkened where Aaron's urine had collected over time. Feces had been cleaned up on the outside, but no one had changed Aaron's underwear. The smell was overwhelming when he stood too close. If not for the fan aimed at Aaron, Clive wouldn't have been able to get near him without holding his breath or wearing a mask.

A table sat against the wall. It held everything Clive needed. The hammer rested beside a large knife, brass knuckles, and smelling salts.

He motioned for the other guards to enter.

"I want everyone to watch our evening's entertainment. Let this be an example of what happens to people who betray me."

Clive made sure the five guards were close. Two of his most trusted men, whom he had used for over a year, stood just inside the door. One man leaned in the doorway against the rock frame, and the other two stood outside, watching from the jagged rock window.

The three-hundred-year-old room made Clive feel he was standing in something Fred Flintstone would have felt right at home. He grinned as he set his cell phone down on the table.

He walked over to Aaron and studied his features.

"Tell me, how did you figure everything out so fast?"

Aaron kept his head down.

Clive didn't hesitate or wait for approval from his men. He had them here to learn something, not to benefit Clive's ego.

He grabbed Aaron's hair and yanked his head back. Tear streaks had made lines in the dirt on Aaron's cheeks. His eyes were half-lidded, and his mouth hung slack as if still drugged. The worst was Aaron's lips. They were puffed up and cracking as if water hadn't passed them in some time.

Clive pulled his hand back and wiped it on his pants.

"Shit … do we have any gloves up here?" he asked.

One of his men ran over and pulled a pair of gloves from the other side of the table.

"Why is he so fucked up?" Clive asked as he slid the gloves on.

"He hasn't eaten in two days, sir. He was heavily drugged for the first day, and even when he screamed for water, we gave him nothing, as you requested."

Clive wondered if he'd done the right thing. He had wanted Aaron cognizant of the interrogation part of his session this evening, but that might be asking too much.

"I have questions that need answering. Get this man water."

He walked in a circle around Aaron, enjoying the breeze from the fan, which alleviated the smell enough to breathe through his nose.

The same man who gave him the gloves bolted back into the room with a bottle of water.

Clive opened it, took a long drink, and then placed it in Aaron's mouth.

"Drink," he said. "It's fresh water."

Aaron moaned and moved his lips. Clive angled his head back and let a little water trickle past Aaron's lips. He coughed and spit it out. Clive tried again. This time, Aaron swallowed, grimacing as he did.

More water flowed down Aaron's throat, coating his lips. Clive pulled the bottle away and set it on the dirt floor when it was almost half gone.

"Better?" he asked.

Aaron opened his eyes enough to look at him.

"You … Clive Baron?"

"You know me?"

It was almost indiscernible, but Clive caught Aaron's nod.

"How do you know me?" Clive asked.

"Your … mother."

"My mother," Clive said as he glanced at the men, a smile playing across his lips. He looked back at Aaron. "You researched my mother or something?" He chuckled.

"No …"

"Then how do you know me through my mother?" Clive

grew serious, tiring fast of Aaron's game.

"She showed me baby pictures of you … the night three of my buddies, and I spent six hours boning her at the whorehouse where she worked in Toronto."

This disgusting waste of human life dared to taunt Clive Baron, billionaire, extraordinaire, esquire. A self-made man, someone people like Aaron depended on. Yet Aaron Stevens not only thwarted him in Toronto, he disrespected him in Greece in front of his men, hard-working men who ate people like Aaron for breakfast.

It was time to get the party started. Aaron would learn quite quickly that he had it backward. He shouldn't have teased the pit bull while *he* was the one chained up.

To the credit of all the men, none made a sound when Aaron disrespected Clive. If they had, they would have joined Aaron.

Clive walked over to the table, examined it briefly, and then selected the hammer.

"Can I have more water?" Aaron asked.

Clive raised his eyebrows. "Sure thing," he said.

He leaned down as if to pick the water up but instead brought the hammer down hard on the top of Aaron's left foot. The sound of the human foot's twenty-six bones breaking was drowned out by Aaron's screams as they pierced the quiet night.

Clive reared back, pleased with his handiwork. He picked the water bottle up and tossed it to the nearest man standing by the door. He wouldn't give Aaron any more water—Aaron wouldn't ever be getting any nourishment. Clive wanted to ensure his men were still watching without making it obvious that he was checking on them. They needed to feel that he trusted them, yet at the same time, every employee needed a minder.

He waited for Aaron to calm down enough to talk. Blood was collected in the hole in the top of Aaron's foot. It reached the top and slipped over the edges, seeping into the dirt below.

To Aaron's credit, he stopped screaming and closed his mouth to a small, clenched circle in which he breathed in and out rapidly. Clive could see that Aaron was trying to avoid passing out.

"Are you ready to talk yet?" Clive asked.

He received no answer from Aaron.

Clive didn't want to wait any longer. "Tell me how you figured everything out. Did you know the Weeks brothers?"

"No," Aaron said, barely over the sound of his heavy breathing. He kept his eyes staring forward at nothing, focusing, breathing.

Clive tapped the tip of the hammer in his free hand as he paced in front of Aaron. "After the idiot Weeks brothers stole my bag at the airport, they opened it and saw secret documents that led to their death. The only problem was I couldn't catch up to them before they went to that strip club and spilled the beans. To protect my secret, anyone who came in contact with Frank and Gary Weeks had to be taken care of." He stopped pacing. "I'm truly sorry that your sister was a slut and gave it up for a couple of dollars at that lap dance palace, but hey, maybe I did her a favor. Maybe I put her out of her misery."

Clive could feel the violence behind Aaron's eyes. There was something about Aaron that made Clive feel like he was standing beside a maniac who, if he weren't tied up, would execute every man in Palamidi, even with his current wounds.

His step almost faltered, but he caught himself.

Too bad I couldn't have met you on different terms. You'd have made a good addition to my team.

"Are you going to tell me how you worked it all out, or were you at the strip club the night the Weeks brothers were there spilling their guts?" He faced his men and raised a finger. "Aha, that must be it. You were there trying to get your sister to dance for you." He knelt on one knee, eye to eye with Aaron. "Look, this doesn't have to be so bad. Tell me what I want to know, and I will end this relatively quickly. Antagonize me, play games, and I will spend the next week breaking all your bones and pulling teeth and fingernails out one by one. Then, the real pain will start. I will remove bones from your body while keeping you alive as long as I can. I hope you understand me. It really is your choice."

Aaron's breathing was leveling off. It didn't seem like he'd run a marathon anymore, just a few flights of stairs.

"Okay, no answer speaks of one thing … defiance. Which tells me you're into pain. You must like it."

Clive lifted the hammer, claw end exposed, and stopped at the peak of the swing as his encrypted cell phone rang on the side table. He was waiting for two different calls on that number: his legal team in Moscow and his RCMP contact in Toronto.

The phone rang again.

"You are one lucky asshole," Clive said under his breath. He set the hammer down by Aaron's chair and moved to the table.

Call display said it was private. He flipped the talk button. "Speak."

"I really shouldn't be doing this—"

"Shut the fuck up," Clive blurted into the phone at the RCMP officer on the other end of the line. "You'll do it, or I'll send a hundred-man team to your fucking house and blow it up *after* they all rape your wife. Now quit whining and tell me what I want to know."

His RCMP contact, Daryl Harper, sounded out of breath. He cleared his throat, coughed, and said, "Nick Sturnam is dead."

"Are you running?"

"No, I just walked up six flights of stairs to get to the roof of the building for privacy. If I got caught talking to you —"

"What happened to Nick?"

"He was beaten up pretty bad. He's missing his left eye completely, like someone pulled it out of his head, and then, it appears he jumped from one of the windows of the hotel. Other than that, the Toronto police don't have much to go on. They're still investigating. All I got was that he showed up in the lobby of the Quality Suites, was given a message from a young male, and then went up the elevator. The message had room 432 written on it. When the police talked to who was in that room at the time, they found a Bulgarian couple on a seven-day trip to Toronto scared shitless."

"Why? How are they involved?"

"Apparently, Nick had shot the door handle off their room, barged in, threatened the man, punched him a few times, and then barged back out. Their English is bad, so communication was difficult."

"And that's it? Nick just decided to kill himself? Doesn't add up." Aaron sat in the wooden chair, his head held high.

"They had a witness who claimed seeing Nick on the second floor, but there was no other damage to the hotel, and no one else reported a scuffle. The cops are coming up blank on this one. Wish I could help more."

"Tell me, did they get a good description of the man who passed the message onto Nick?" Clive asked.

"The guy in the lobby described him as mid-twenties, fit, athletic, and in a hurry. The report said he had dark, wavy hair, but that's all I got. Is it important?"

"No, it's fine. I got everything I needed. Thanks, Daryl. You will be rewarded for this."

"Just don't call me anymore—"

Clive hung up before he heard the rest. He set his phone on the table and collected himself for what he had to do next. He studied Aaron's wavy, dark hair and athletic build and started putting it all together.

"Why were you at the Quality Suites Hotel in Toronto the other night?"

Aaron looked up at Clive, then glanced away. It was enough to show that Aaron knew exactly what Clive was talking about. It was Aaron at that hotel. Aaron had given Nick a note. But why? Did Nick get sloppy? Where did Aaron get his information?

"Who the hell are you?" Clive asked.

He was genuinely getting concerned. Could Aaron really just be the brother of a dead whore? Or were Joanne and Aaron Stevens covers for something deeper?

Paranoia settled over him. What if he was being watched right now?

He turned to the five men attending the evening's performance and motioned with the hammer.

"Which of you went to the hotel in Toronto with Nick?"

One of the men outside the window raised a hand like he was in school. "It was me."

"Come in and tell me what happened."

The man nodded and moved away from the window. He eased past the other men and moved closer to Clive. "Nick followed him," he nodded toward Aaron, "and when we saw him run into the hotel, all four of us followed. Nick talked to the clerk at the front desk, and then he told me to wait behind Aaron's car in case they missed him in the hotel. If anything went wrong, I was supposed to grab Aaron and drive him immediately to the Island Airport, where I would find a plane waiting to bring Aaron here."

"Why did you come alone?" Clive asked. "Did something go wrong?"

The man nodded.

"Can you be more specific?" Clive could tell his guard thought he did the right thing, but under the stress of interrogation, he shook like a paint mixer.

"I broke Aaron's wrist and knocked him out. After shoving him into the back of his car, someone on the second floor of the hotel opened their room window and shouted at me to stop. I saw at least two different men, young men, stick their heads out. Since I thought we had been made, I immediately delivered Aaron to the airport."

"You did good. You did the right thing. Now, go and do a perimeter check. Make sure we're alone. If Aaron had people waiting at the hotel to help him, maybe he has people watching us right now." He motioned to the men to go, then pointed at the guy who brought him, Aaron. "You stay behind and watch the door. Have your weapons out, safeties off."

The men nodded and moved away, disappearing into the darkness.

"Tell me what you know, Mr. Stevens. I'm serious now. I want to know who you work for."

Aaron slowly met Clive's gaze. "The agency I work for has everything they need on you. We know about the *vodka*. We know about the murders. Only the best men to come out of our facility are hunting you right now. Clive Baron, you will pay for your crimes whether I live or die. That was my mission. I accepted it with honor to live or die bringing you in." He spit to clear the saliva building up around his teeth. "I'm just surprised you sent such amateurs after me, like those two at the strip club and the *hitman* that followed me to the hotel. Come on, I thought you had more money than that." Aaron turned away and mumbled something else.

Clive didn't believe a word Aaron was saying, yet it all made sense. Jackson and Hugh were ex-Mossad. They were two of the best men at hand-to-hand combat and guerrilla warfare he'd ever met. Yet Aaron fell Hugh with one hit, according to Jackson's call days ago after picking Gary Weeks up.

Nick Sturnam was a career sniper and hitman, yet Nick was dead, and Jackson and Hugh were in a Toronto jail. Aaron sat in front of him, still alive.

He had to think. He moved to the table out of Aaron's view. What organization would have Aaron as an employee? Was it an international group or the Canadian Joint Task Force 2? He knew the JTF2 was an elite special force primarily tasked with counterterrorism operations. One of the best special operations forces in the world, they were known to work internationally with Britain's Special Air Service, Poland's GROM, and America's Delta Force. He'd heard many good things about the JTF2, but most of what they did was highly classified, and even with his numerous contacts, Clive didn't know much about them.

"What did you mumble a moment ago?" Clive asked.

"Nothing."

Clive's patience had waned. He moved behind Aaron, lifted the hammer, and brought it down on Aaron's unbroken hand. It snapped sideways. The bones broke loud enough to hear, music to Clive's ears. Now, Aaron could only walk on one foot, and he couldn't use either hand. Within the next few minutes, unless Aaron answered questions to Clive's satisfaction, he would never walk again. A hammer could do wonders on Aaron's spine.

I'll break a bunch of vertebrae, and we'll see who has the last laugh.

"No more playing games. Answer me seriously, or you will be a broken pile of bones within minutes."

Aaron's screams subsided when he passed out again.

"Shit."

He grabbed the water bottle, opened it, and poured it over Aaron's head. He didn't stir.

"Smelling salts," a voice said behind him.

Clive's man pointed toward the table.

"Right." Clive retrieved the smelling salts and waved them under Aaron's nose. Aaron snapped his head back, moaning.

"And we're back." Clive clapped his hands. "Now, what did you say under your breath?"

Aaron struggled with the ropes.

"Impressive, but you won't be able to escape. Just answer my questions."

"I said, *fucking amateur*."

Clive guffawed. "You've got to be kidding me. *I'm* the amateur? Who is sitting tied up in the chair? Who has numerous broken bones—"

Gunfire cut him off, followed by another weapon being fired. Then, two more in rapid succession.

Clive ducked as if bullets flew above his head. "What the fuck is happening?" he shouted at the guard by the door. "Go find out."

"But sir … leave you alone in here?"

"Go. I'm armed. Report back at once."

"Yes, sir." The guard jumped past the door and was swallowed by the dark.

"Is that your rescue team?" he asked Aaron.

Aaron nodded.

"If anyone tries to come through that door, I will execute you. They will have no one to save."

Clive moved around behind Aaron and waited, listening. After a full minute, another weapon discharged, and then another. Clive jumped each time.

He had been close to death for many years. Death that he caused with his own hands. But men shooting at him always made him mess with his shorts. He hated the thought of a stray bullet punching through his leg or, worse, his chest.

A man screamed in the dark outside the room, somewhere to the right. Sweat trickled down Clive's back. He wiped his forehead.

Why is everything falling apart? Where did I go wrong?

He picked up his cell phone from the table and called his driver.

"Come to the entrance and pick me up in five minutes."

"I'll be there."

He hung up and listened to the still night. He heard nothing except for the soft murmurs from Aaron.

Something moved in the darkness outside the door.

"Hello?" Clive waited for a moment. "Anybody there?"

Silence filled the cavernous room other than the fan still blowing. Clive couldn't take it anymore. He turned the fan off and moved to the wall beside the door, resting his shoulder against it. He heard nothing coming from the outside.

From this distance, it looked like Aaron was fighting to stay awake.

Clive lifted his gun and aimed it at Aaron.

"You have caused me too much trouble. I will probably have to spend the next half a year fixing everything you've done. That will cost me a lot of money, but it will be money I still have because no one will know my secret. No one will ever know my secret." He placed both hands on the weapon to better his aim. "Goodbye, Aaron Stevens. Say hello to your whore of a sister when you see her."

Clive fired his weapon, the bullet entering Aaron's lower chest near the bottom of the ribcage. He adjusted his aim higher and fired again. This time, a small circle formed near the center of Aaron's pectoral muscle, just below the left collarbone.

Aaron's body jerked with each hit, and then his head slumped down impossibly low. From where Clive stood, it didn't appear Aaron was breathing.

Outside, he made his way to his car, which would take him to a private hotel. He would plan his escape to another country where extradition proved difficult and spend six months working out any issues these recent events had caused.

But first, he needed to get out of Palamidi. He had no idea who his men were shooting at or if another strike team was advancing on Palamidi. He couldn't tell where anyone was in the darkness under the crescent moon.

He stayed close to the stone wall and moved slowly to avoid catching anyone's eye. When he made it to the main door without interruption, he knew he was seconds from being home free.

Palamidi remained silent. He couldn't hear the waves of the Aegean Sea two hundred meters below. Nothing moved. It was like his men had disappeared.

Maybe they had silenced the aggressors and returned to the bastion where he held Aaron. He had no idea what had happened and no way to find out in the dark. Aaron Stevens was dead. That was all he cared about. Regrettably, he had wanted more time with Aaron, but the deed was done. It was time to move on, finish cleaning up the mess in Toronto, and return to handling day-to-day business.

Past the main doors, he made sure his feet came down quietly on the concrete. The lights out, the Mercedes idled quietly twenty feet in front of him.

Was the attack only on the inside of Palamidi tonight, or was his car compromised? The only way to determine if the car was compromised was to walk up and check.

He raised his weapon and walked toward the car. He moved along the side and aimed the gun at the driver.

It was the same driver as before. The driver jumped in his seat and dropped the paperback he'd been reading, raising his hands.

Clive lowered the weapon to his side and told the man to drop the window.

"Nerves got the better of me. You ready?" Clive asked.

The driver nodded.

Clive got in the back.

"Let's go."

The driver started down the road. Clive set the gun beside him in the seat and wiped his face with both hands. He would have to send a cleanup crew to Palamidi tomorrow to remove all traces of his presence. He only had the fortress for another day and had no idea how many men were dead.

The Mercedes moved slowly down the winding road along the hillside overlooking Nafplio. Clive breathed a sigh of relief at the city's shining lights below.

It was over. All he had to do was clean up. That wouldn't be so bad. He'd made it.

He leaned back, breathing easier.

A rock the size of a huge brick smashed into the windshield, so suddenly, Clive didn't have time to register what it was. At the same time, a crazed man ran into the road from the right, carrying another rock over his head.

The driver hit the brakes and swerved hard to the left. The Mercedes went airborne, 150 meters above Nafplio. No guardrail stopped the car. No trees slowed its descent.

The Mercedes tumbled over and over as it fell, first breaking Clive's legs and then arms as he was tossed about like he was in a washing machine. The driver's screams ceased after the fifth rotation.

Clive's neck snapped on the sixth rotation, ceasing his screams, too.

Chapter 28

Aaron woke to a bright light. He kept his eyes closed, but the light invaded his eyelids. He tried to turn his head but was rewarded with shouting.

Numerous people surrounded him. He could feel it. He could also feel pain.

"More anesthetic, get me more anesthetic …" a man's voice shouted from far away.

Aaron faded, losing the light, losing the sounds of the people.

He faded.

Then he was gone.

***

Movement close. Aaron detected someone near him.

Defense mechanisms forced his eyes open fast. He

slammed them shut as the light stung.

He moaned. He couldn't move. Every slight adjustment caused pain.

Someone spoke, but he hadn't paid attention. He listened again.

"How are you feeling?"

Aaron tried to open his eyes to a slit. The room came into focus slowly.

A hospital room. Dark blue walls. Concrete. Not modern. Tubes and wires hung over his head.

A man in a lab coat appeared.

"How are you feeling?"

Aaron tried to answer, but his throat was parched. The man in the lab coat disappeared. He heard water running or being poured. The man came back into view, a glass of water in his hands, a straw bent toward Aaron's mouth.

"Here, try some of this …"

Aaron opened his cracked lips and winced.

How long have I been out?

He sipped the water and almost choked. After getting the first few sips down, it became easier.

The man didn't answer him. He must've said it in his head.

"How long …" he stopped. His voice was huskier, darker. He didn't recognize it.

"Take it easy." The man placed the water out of sight. "We have plenty of time to talk. You've been beat up pretty bad, but you're on the mend now." He smiled. "You're a fighter, you know that?"

"Where … am I?"

"In a hospital in Nafplio, Greece."

A beeping increased from somewhere in the room as his heart rate sped up.

"Stay calm. It's all okay now. There's no threat here."

The beeping leveled after a moment and slowed again.

Aaron's eyes adjusted to the light. He tried to take more of the room in, but his chest was secured to the bed in some way. None of his limbs responded except for his right leg, which wasn't tied down.

"What happened?"

"You'll be all right, but it'll take time. Your hands will heal well. We fixed both breaks in the wrists and wired and cast them. In a few months, they'll be back to 99 percent. Your left foot has also been repaired and cast, but I don't see you walking on it for a few months."

The doctor paused, a grim expression crossing his face.

"What?" Aaron asked.

"It wasn't the breaks that concerned me. It was the two gunshot wounds."

Aaron blinked slowly and deeply, tired of talking already.

The doctor continued. "One of the bullets entered through your pectoral muscle, passed through your rib cage, missed everything important, and exited out your back, south of your shoulder blade. The exit wound took some patching, but you won't be pitching any baseball games for a year at least."

Aaron closed his eyes. He'd never had wounds so extensive before. The worst was a few broken fingers in competitions years ago when he was still learning the martial arts, but that was it.

"The other bullet was just under your ribcage. The problem with that one is it grazed your stomach and ruptured your spleen. The spleen helps rid your body of bacterial infections. We're monitoring every few hours." The doctor stopped and grabbed a clipboard from somewhere at the end of the bed. "Other than that, you're a specimen of perfect health."

Aaron opened and closed his heavy eyelids. Sleep called him. He didn't have the energy to ask any more questions even though he wanted to know what happened on Palamidi and what happened to Clive Baron. Were the police looking for Aaron, showing up in a foreign hospital without a passport, beaten up, broken, and shot?

The doctor spoke as Aaron faded in and out.

"Your friends are here. They just went out for lunch. I'll have them come by and tell you what they know …"

Friends? What friends? The police? Clive's men?

Aaron fought sleep. He needed to know who his friends were. But there was nothing he could do. Sleep enveloped him, wrapped his wounded body in a tight blanket, and drifted him off to nothingness for ten more hours.

***

Alex's voice. Then Benjamin's, and finally, Daniel's. They were talking about money. Who would pay back who and when?

Aaron came back to consciousness, listening to them debate the point.

"I'll pay it," Aaron said. "Just be quiet …"

He opened his eyes and squinted until his three friends came into focus. "Water?"

"Here, drink this," Daniel said.

After he got some moisture in his throat again, the doctor visited briefly, asked a few routine questions, and left the four to talk.

Aaron adjusted the bed as high as possible without causing too much pain.

"Why were you arguing … about money?" Aaron asked.

Benjamin glanced at his friends and gave Aaron a sheepish grin. "Alex lent us the money to fly here. We were talking about how to pay it back."

"Why are you guys … here?" Aaron asked, surprised at how raspy his voice was. "How did you know?"

"I'll tell you." Daniel cleared his throat and crossed his legs like he was getting settled to make a speech. "It all started at the hotel. When you told me to research Clive Baron, I found out a lot of stuff, most of it bad. When these guys showed up, we talked, but we couldn't agree on anything." He leaned forward and gestured with his hands. "You have to understand, we were scared. Your sister had been murdered, and you were going up against a billionaire. We thought that if we said we wouldn't help, you would go to the police and seek protection or something." He looked at the brothers for support and then back at Aaron. "We didn't think you'd continue alone." He paused and swallowed hard, fidgeting with the cuff of his pant leg.

Aaron waited for him to continue.

"We decided at the last minute that we had to help. Alex and I stuck our heads out the hotel window to yell at you to come back to the room. As you got to your car, we saw some guy jump up and club you over the head and then shove you into your own car. We yelled at him, but he drove off in your car. As we tried to leave the room, a man with a large bandage over one eye was standing in the hall with a gun aimed at us."

Daniel high-fived Alex.

"What was that for?" Aaron asked.

"Alex snuck around me and snapped the guy's wrist in half while shoving the barrel of the gun up. It happened so fast even I didn't see Alex coming."

Aaron smiled. It was his first smile in days.

"Anyway," Daniel continued, "we figured this bandaged guy would know something about where the other guy was taking you. It didn't take too much persuasion—although he ended up with seven broken fingers before he told us all the details—and then we drove across to Toronto's main airport and bought tickets for the next flight to Athens. When we landed in Greece, we took a bus to Nafplio the same day. It was the day they started your interrogation. Boy, were we happy we weren't late for the party."

"What happened to the bandaged guy?" Aaron asked, remembering something from Clive's cell phone call in prison.

"We gave him an option. We would break all his toes so he couldn't run when the police came to the hotel, or he could jump from the hotel window and take his chances. We thought he'd break an ankle or a leg if he jumped. Well, the guy decided to jump. Who knew he'd land wrong and snap his neck."

"How did you get into the fortress?"

"We waited until the sun dropped, scaled a small wall at the far end of Palamidi, it was only about ten feet high, and used all our ninja skills," the three of them snickered like little kids, "to take out the guys who had weapons. Clive proved the trickiest. Once we had taken out the guards, we heard a car coming up the road. I asked Alex to stay at the main gate to see who it was and to stop Clive if he was trying to leave. Benjamin and I found you unconscious and bleeding. Somehow, Clive got past us on our way to you. We called for an ambulance, and then we heard a horrific crash." He looked over at Alex. "You can continue from here."

Alex nodded, cracked his knuckles, tilted his head back and forth, and said, "I saw Clive get in a Mercedes. I couldn't stop him, so I threw a big rock at the windshield and ran out in front of the car. It swerved and went off the road. I had no idea it would catch fire and explode halfway down the hill. The fire at that hour helped emergency services get to us faster. It's pretty dry here in Greece this time of year, and with a fire that close to the city … well, let's just say they were true to their Olympian form in handling the fire like Spartans."

Always the gamer, Aaron thought.

Daniel jumped back in. "We didn't kill any guards, just put them to sleep. When the police arrived, they arrested everyone but us. As far as I know, they've all been charged with kidnapping, assault, and attempted murder. Clive's accident has been classified as just that, an accident."

Aaron couldn't believe it. His sister's murderer was dead, and it was with the help of his students and his friends.

He looked away to hide the tears that crept past his eyes. An uncomfortable silence filled the room.

Alex broke it. "You okay?"

Aaron nodded. "Just give me a moment."

He heard one of them move away. Someone cleared their throat. Aaron wiped at the tears and looked back at them.

"I'm sorry. I should be more grateful. It's just …"

"What?" Benjamin asked.

"It's just that I've lost Joanne. I wanted to make her killer pay. I wanted to hunt Clive down and make him feel it," he stopped to collect himself. The pain was returning in his chest near his bullet wounds. He wondered if talking had re-opened the wounds. "It's just, I failed her. When I needed to stand up, I fell."

"You know the proverb," Daniel said. "Fall seven times, stand eight."

Aaron nodded. "When these guys took me, I knew I was finished. I gave up. I would be dead right now if it weren't for you guys." He winced. "Although with the pain I'm in, maybe dead is a good option. At least I'd be with my sister."

"I'll get the doctor." Alex jumped to his feet.

"Hold up," Aaron said. He clenched his teeth and waited for the pain to subside. Alex reached the hospital room door and held the handle, waiting for Aaron to speak.

"I want you guys to know that," Aaron started, "you're my family now. You guys are my brothers. What you did for me, even family members wouldn't do. Who needs family when I have people like you in my life?"

Alex opened the door.

"When my parents walked away all those years ago, I was alone. But now I'm walking away from them. I'm letting it go. There's solitude and comfort there. Thank you for allowing me to see that."

The pain took over, and Alex slipped out the door. Aaron looked at his casts as his eyes watered. He knew he would walk again. He would fight again. He would live. If not for himself, for Joanne.

Clive was dead, the nightmare over.
Aaron wondered if Clive's secret had died with him.

251

Chapter 29

FOUR MONTHS LATER ...

Alex insisted on pushing the wheelchair. Benjamin and Daniel followed in their oversized suits, trying to look respectable.

The courtroom was packed. Dozens of people had come to see what would happen.

John Ashcroft, the man Aaron had beaten up and put in a coma, had awakened six weeks ago. He had called for his wife and asked for her forgiveness and a divorce. Aaron heard that the man didn't feel worthy of marriage anymore. He called to see his daughter, but she still refused to see him.

John asked to see Aaron Stevens, but his lawyer denied that request.

Then, John Ashcroft waived all charges. He claimed he wouldn't show up in court as the complainant. He did not want to press charges.

When his lawyer tried to convince him otherwise, John said he would attend court and tell the judge that he had asked his Shotokan karate teacher, Aaron Stevens, for private lessons. They had been sparring, which was usual in the dojo, and John had willingly pushed Aaron to spar as if they were street fighting. Things got out of hand, but that was it. He would claim that Aaron was his friend and that he forgave him. It was over. Let it go.

The lawyers had met, and today's court date was only a formality.

All charges were dismissed. He was a free man with no criminal record. He already had designs on a new dojo. A bigger, better building where Alex, Benjamin, and Daniel would take on teaching roles until Aaron had healed enough to come on full-time.

They exited the courthouse, turned the corner by the stairs, and Alex rolled Aaron down the wheelchair ramp.

It was his last week in a chair. His physiotherapist said he would be taking the chair back. Aaron was walking well enough on his own. The chair was lent to him only for his court appearance.

At the bottom of the ramp, a man stepped out of the shadows and called Aaron's name. The chair stopped, and Alex moved in front of Aaron.

"It's okay, Alex. That's Folley. He's a cop."

Alex moved aside, cracking his knuckles. Aaron caught Daniel wrapping an arm around Alex's shoulders to rein him in.

"Aaron, I wanted to congratulate you. I'm happy to see the charges dropped. It was the right thing to do."

Aaron nodded his thanks.

"I found a few things out recently that I thought you should know."

"Like what?" Aaron asked.

The sun beat down between them, but Aaron still shivered in his chair. It was late November, the air crisp in downtown Toronto. Cabs honked their horns, cars raced by, and police sirens wailed in the distance. Life in Toronto stopped for no one.

"We discovered Clive Baron's secret."

"I'm not sure I'm interested anymore."

"Bullshit," Folley said. "I know you. I saw what you did with that Rubik's Cube. You like a puzzle. You want to know as much as I did."

Aaron didn't move or ask his brothers to move him.

"Clive owned grain alcohol distilleries in the States. He was meeting scientists in Toronto to help perfect his recipes."

Aaron squinted in the sun, listening. So far, he couldn't see what secret would be worth killing for.

"In a nutshell, his company, the grain alcohol distillers, would dye their alcohol blue to make it look like windshield washer fluid, and the barrels were labeled as such. Then, they were shipped to Russia, avoiding all duties levied on imported liquor. Inspectors in Russia would see the liquid was blue and labeled as windshield washer fluid and then let it in the country."

Folley stopped to cough and then continued. "Once it was in Russia, there was no way to tell whether the taxes had been paid or not. The smugglers, Clive's men, then removed the coloring using special instructions from the scientists Clive employed for this task. The contraband alcohol had flavor added and was bottled. Then, it was sold to unsuspecting retailers across Russia through a massive distribution center in Moscow as genuine vodka called *Absolutely Russian Vodka*. He kept his actual alcohol shipments to ten percent of his overall imports so no one would question his activities."

Folley pulled a piece of paper out of his pocket. He talked while keeping his head down. "Did you know that the average Russian citizen drinks up to twelve gallons of vodka annually? That's more spirits than any other nation."

"No, I didn't know that," Aaron said.

Alex made to move the wheelchair around but stopped when Folley raised his arm, extending the paper to Aaron.

"Here, this is for you."

No one attempted to take it from Folley.

"What is it?" Aaron asked.

"It's the information on your parents. I found them."

Aaron wasn't sure he heard him right. "What?"

"Your parents. I found them. They're still alive and living ten minutes' drive from here. I know why they walked away from you and your sister all those years ago. Everything's here on this paper if you decide to contact them."

Aaron stared at the paper, not allowing his expression to change. He had waited for this day for so many years, and now that it was finally here, he just stared.

"Let me tell you something, Folley."

The cop lowered his hand, the paper clenched in his fingers and waited.

"One day, the Buddha was teaching his ideas on a hillside. A man showed up and started yelling at him, calling him crazy and shouting that he shouldn't be filling people's heads with such nonsense. The Buddha turned to the angry man and asked if he had a white piece of paper. The man was befuddled, but he produced a piece of paper and handed it to the Buddha, who accepted it and promptly handed it back. The man asked why he did that. Why take it and then hand it back? The Buddha explained that the man's anger was the paper, and that was what the Buddha was doing with the man's anger. He was letting him keep it."

Aaron turned his chair around on his own and pushed the wheels. "Goodbye, Folley. May my parents rest in peace."

"But Aaron, they're your family."

Aaron stopped his wheelchair and half turned back. "No, Folley." He pointed to Alex, Daniel, and Benjamin. "These men are my family. They were there when I needed them. They took risks for me and stood by me. That's family. It has nothing to do with blood or DNA and everything to do with humanity."

He pushed away again. As his brothers followed, he shouted over his shoulder to Folley, "Solve the Rubik's Cube, and you'll know what I'm talking about. Life is a puzzle, and you have to work it out for yourself, and only you can work it out."

About Jonas Saul

Jonas Saul is the bestselling author of the Sarah Roberts
Series—more than two million sold!—and has written
and published over sixty thrillers. After acquiring an
agent, he signed several deals in Los Angeles, with
MadRiver Pictures optioning his Sarah Roberts Series—
over forty books!—(currently in development).

Jonas has often outranked Stephen King and Dean

Koontz on Amazon over the past decade. He's regularly invited to be a guest speaker, teacher, or workshop presenter at international writing conferences and film festivals worldwide. He hosts an annual writer's retreat in Greece, where he currently lives. He focuses his teaching on how to get tension and emotion in every scene, on every page, how he made it as a creator/writer, the path to success in this business, and the pitfalls to avoid. He also hosts a reading retreat in Greece with guest authors, yoga retreats, and hiking retreats. Visit the Imagine Greece Retreats website at www.imaginegreeceretreats.com, or email him directly to discuss an opportunity to join one of the retreats at jonas@imaginegreeceretreats.com.

Jonas is also a professional freelance editor. He works for several publishers and does private editing for clients, with many testimonials on his website at www.imaginepress.org, which details each author's response to Jonas's editing skills. Email Jonas directly for an editing quote at editor@imaginepress.org.

To book Jonas for a speaking engagement at a writer's conference/festival, to have him on your jury at a film festival, or even to say hello, email Jonas directly at jonassaul@icloud.com.

For updates on releases, hit the "Follow" button on Amazon or Bookbub, and join Jonas on Facebook, where he's most active.

Contact Jonas Saul

Linktree: Find me here

Email: jonassaul@icloud.com